## "Have you been happy, Nell?"

Her mouth went dry, her pulse began racing wildly. It was as if the past three years had never been and she was once again his darling Nell. Her head was bent, and she felt his warm breath stirring the wisps of hair on her neck.

"Of course I have," she answered.

The heat of his breath upon her neck increased, and a shiver coursed the length of her spine as his warm lips pressed into the softness of her neck. She let the delight of it overwhelm her for one brief, delicious moment.

"Oh, Nell, Nell," he whispered.

Her eyes closed as his finger lightly traced the line of her delicate cheek beside her defiant, upturned nose. He drew her against him and, as if possessing a will of its own, her head tilted back to meet his kiss.

Dear Reader:

After more than one year of publication, SECOND CHANCE AT LOVE has a lot to celebrate. Not only has it become firmly established as a major line of paperback romances, but response from our readers also continues to be warm and enthusiastic. Your letters keep pouring in—and we love receiving them. We're getting to know you—your likes and dislikes—and want to assure you that your contribution does make a difference.

As we work hard to offer you better and better SECOND CHANCE AT LOVE romances, we're especially gratified to hear that you, the reader, are rating us higher and higher. After all, our success depends on *you*. We're pleased that you enjoy our books and that you appreciate the extra effort our writers and staff put into them. Thanks for spreading the good word about SECOND CHANCE AT LOVE and for giving us your loyal support. Please keep your suggestions and comments coming!

With warm wishes,

*Ellen Edwards*

Ellen Edwards
SECOND CHANCE AT LOVE
The Berkley/Jove Publishing Group
200 Madison Avenue
New York, NY 10016

## Second Chance at Love

### REGENCY

# AN IMPROPER BETROTHMENT
# HENRIETTA HOUSTON

**SECOND CHANCE AT LOVE
BOOK**

AN IMPROPER BETROTHMENT

First edition published September 1982

First printing

"Second Chance at Love" and the butterfly emblem are trademarks belonging to Jove Publications, Inc.

Printed in the United States of America

Second Chance at Love books are published by
The Berkley/Jove Publishing Group
200 Madison Avenue, New York, NY 10016

For Mom and Dad,
with Love

# - 1 -

ELEANOR TRANT'S LOVELY face rivaled a summer storm cloud. Her brows drew together over snapping green eyes. Her red lips were thrust out in unspeakable anger. Copper curls trailed across her cheeks in disordered waves as she strode back and forth in the morning room in front of a young woman huddled on the threadbare sofa.

"How could you, Elizabeth?" Eleanor halted to demand again in a voice barely under control. "How *could* you?"

Elizabeth's upturned face was devoid of color. Her lips quivered in an effort to reply. Her fingers played nervously with the bow of the chip-hat that she'd tossed wrathfully beside her. Then she began to twist the heavy folds of her cloak. Tears welled up within her light blue eyes and rolled sadly down her creamy cheeks.

Seeing this, the thundercloud faded from Eleanor's face. Shoving aside her traveling cloak and bonnet, she sank down next to the younger girl. "I'm not angry at you, Beth," she said, "truly I'm not. No one could ever be angry at you, Beth, dearest." She gathered her unresisting sister into her arms and explained gently, "It's simply that I do not understand. You and that—*that man!*" Fury crept back into her voice, sending a shiver through Elizabeth. "It passes all bounds!"

1

"Oh, Nell," Beth sobbed as she buried her soft brown curls into her sister's comforting shoulder, "you know I wouldn't hurt you for all the world!"

"Shh, no, of course not," Nell murmured soothingly. She knew full well that Beth was incapable of deliberately bringing pain to anyone. But she could not deny that beneath her own shock and anger there drummed a steady, dull aching that she knew only too well. Three years had not dimmed her ability to suffer such heartache. The last two days had been more than proof of that.

As her sister continued to cry quietly, Nell vividly recalled that first stunned moment of disbelief she had experienced upon reading her mother's letter. At first she had stood stiffly, unable to breathe, to think, even to feel. A furious frenzy had followed, resulting in the destruction of two vases and a porcelain figurine before Miss Poole had captured her and rocked her with much the same consoling whispers that Eleanor now used to comfort Beth. After that, of course, had come the dreadful dull but constant thudding of a heart she had long since believed safely beyond such misery.

Dear, sweet, loyal Drusilla Poole! Nell thought with a sad smile. Knowing that Nell would not be capable of instructing a class in their small but exclusive school for young ladies, Miss Poole had not only agreed that Nell post down to London, she had insisted on it. Within hours of first reading her mother's letter, Nell had been seated alone with her memories on the squabs of a post-chaise headed south. Unfolding the sheet she had crumpled in her rage, Nell had read it over until the searing words were branded into her heart.

"Of course," her mother had written in her lazy scrawl, "you will rejoice with us in our happy news. Our little Beth has accepted the suit of Sir Charles Grayson! Thus, despite the difficulties of the past,"—for which Nell mentally substituted, *your willfulness*—"we Trants are, after all, to be allied with the Graysons of Graveley Hall."

Even now, holding her sister's trembling form, Nell could not believe it. How could they all be so foolish, so insensitive, as to countenance a betrothment between her sister and her own former fiancé?

When Beth stopped crying, Nell gently released her and

moved restlessly to stand before the unsteady, wavering flames in the room's tiny boxlike fireplace. Holding her hands out, though knowing nothing could warm her, she questioned bitterly, "Am I to assume that you love him?"

What little color had inched its way into Elizabeth's round face now fled. "Oh, Nell, *no!*"

The involuntary exclamation brought Nell's piercing green eyes around to probe deeply into Beth's gaze. The younger woman shook her brown curls in denial and clutched again at the much-abused cloak.

"What then?" demanded Nell with impatience. "What possible reason could you have for agreeing to wed such an out-and-out rake?"

"Mama," breathed Beth, shrinking visibly beneath the unbending force of her elder sister's wrathful look.

"Oh, of course, Mama would be thrilled! But even she must have had a good reason to disregard the inevitable talk that will begin once this news is out." Nell's head was bent toward the fire again, hiding from Beth's view the traces of hurt etched into the thin, pale cheeks.

"Papa," came the whispered reply. Again Nell shot her a searching look and, summoning up her courage, Beth took a deep breath and added, "A-after Grandmama left her money to you and you j-jilted Sir Charles—"

"It was a mutual dissolvement of our betrothal!" Nell cut in through clenched teeth.

"Y-yes. Well, Papa seemed to think that the only way out of our debts was to—to speculate," Beth continued tremulously. "Mama explained it all to me, you see, when Sir Charles approached them."

"Approached them?" Once again Nell scrutinized Beth's timid face. "Did he not declare his love to you beforehand?"

"Oh, this is not to be a love match," her sister explained eagerly. "You see, Nell, Sir Charles needs a wife. He told Papa that he is no longer in his salad days—"

"That at least is true!" Nell tartly interrupted. "He's thirty-two if he's a day!"

"H-he said it was time for him to take a wife and that—that I should do quite well."

"And it was flattery such as this that led to your acceptance."

Beth flinched under her sister's sarcasm. A quivering

hand rose as if to fend off further blows and Nell, instantly contrite, covered her cheeks with her hands.

"Forgive me, dearest! I am being a beast, I know." She lowered her hands and turned to the fire. "What did Mama tell you?"

"She said that Papa had not been . . . had not speculated wisely and that Sir Charles's proposal was a gift from God," Beth answered in her breathy voice. "She said that if you had not . . . what I mean—"

Nell broke in with a bitter laugh. "Don't worry, Beth. I know full well that Mama has never forgiven me for not going through with the wedding! After all, wealthy, arrogant rakes are difficult to come by as husbands these days."

"Oh, Nell, please don't!" her sister begged, covering her face with her hands. "I can't bear it when you look like that! So—so scornful and contemptuous."

A heavy sigh dropped between them. After a time Eleanor said flatly, "So you are to wed Sir Charles to save the Trants from ruin."

"Y-yes."

"But do you *want* to marry Sir Charles?" she inquired, regarding Beth from beneath red-gold lashes.

"Y-yes," Beth answered bravely, fixing her cornflower-blue eyes upon the lap of her pink cambric day dress. But the fiery flush that cloaked her neck and cheeks belied her reply and Nell's green eyes narrowed with suspicion.

"Don't be a goose, Beth! You can't expect to find happiness with a man of Grayson's stamp!"

Keeping her head bent over her lap, Beth did not respond to this charge. Sighing again, Nell picked up the iron poker and stoked up the fire. When it roared back to life, she dropped the poker onto its stand with a metallic clang that emphasized the thick silence between them. Eleanor stood staring, mesmerized, into the blaze.

"Beth," she said finally without removing her eyes from the fire, "I want you to realize what you are doing. That's why I posted down here from Norfolk in such haste. You do not understand what Grayson is like."

"I know his reputation," Beth replied. "And I don't mind—truly, I do not!—if he continues to have . . . to have mistresses and such things."

"Beyond his reputation, Beth," Nell said sharply, "there is the man himself. He is rude, arrogant, insufferably proud, tyrannical. How could you possibly accept such a man for your husband?"

"Perhaps for my charm of manner?" suggested a deep voice behind them.

Her heart pounding, Eleanor spun around to stare into blue eyes that seemed to bore right through her. From beneath heavy lids his penetrating gaze ran the length of her tall, thin figure, making Nell all too aware of the rumpled state of her plain brown traveling gown, the wild disarray of her dark red curls, and the shadow of fatigue beneath her large green eyes. He watched with distinct amusement as the first dull gloss of shock within those eyes blazed into a furious gleam of anger.

Managing, however, to keep her voice coolly disdainful, Nell remarked, "Your *lack* of manners, you must mean. I did not hear you knock, Sir Charles."

"That is because, my dear Miss Trant," he responded, unperturbed, "I did not do so."

With a sure, easy step, he crossed to take the shaking hand Elizabeth extended to him. Bending the length of his broad form to drop a careless kiss upon it, he quickly released it and straightened. He smiled lazily at the hostile beauty standing rigidly before the fireplace, then mused aloud, but as if to himself, "Now, I wonder, ought I to begin addressing you as 'sister'?"

"Oh, please," Beth broke in hurriedly, "I'm sorry to say, Sir Charles, that Mama and Papa are gone out."

The note of appeal in her voice drew his attention, and Sir Charles scanned the whitened face of his betrothed, the mocking smile lingering on his lips. "But I did not come to see your parents, my love," he said.

The loverlike tone struck Nell palpably. She felt a stab of pain and looked down slowly to discover her nails digging into the soft flesh of her palms. Unclenching her fists, she said as evenly as she could manage, "I do not think, Sir Charles, that you shall need to address me as anything at all. My stay in town is but a brief one."

"Ah, yes," he drawled casually in a voice that held a hint of underlying steel, "the school in Norfolk. The fulfilling career that meant so much to you. I confess I am surprised to find you were able to tear yourself away for even so much as a day."

Each word lashed out at her, and Nell found her hands curling into fists once again.

"It was, of course, difficult," she returned in withering accents, "but Miss Poole will see that the school is smoothly managed during the short time I shall be away."

"The ever-capable Miss Poole." The lids dropped over his eyes but not before she had seen the contempt in them. "And she is, I trust, as cold-blooded as ever?"

"Miss Poole is not cold!" Nell denied heatedly. "She is a dear, dear friend and one without whom—"

"Your life would have been vastly different," he finished harshly.

"Why, you fatuous, conceited—"

"Still dedicated to spinsterhood, is she, our Miss Poole?" Sir Charles interrupted with calm interest.

The heat of her anger rekindled Nell's emerald eyes and flooded her face with a becoming flush. Suddenly Elizabeth jumped up, fear contorting her own generally pleasant features.

"Please, Sir Charles, won't you be seated? I'll get some tea or—or—"

"That's quite all right, Elizabeth," Nell said quickly. "Since I have but just arrived, I shall retire to my room. I am certain you and your fiancé have much to discuss."

She started for the door, but Sir Charles stepped lithely into her path, blocking her way with his implacable presence. "Perhaps, Miss Beth," he began calmly, "you should see about that tea. Your sister obviously needs the comfort of a cup after her long journey."

Hovering hesitantly, her unhappy indecision plain to see, Beth cast a pleading look at her sister. Gritting her teeth, Nell capitulated. "Yes, Beth, I do believe a cup of tea would be refreshing," she said mendaciously as she turned back to the fire.

Screwing her eyes tightly shut, as if to blot out all that was happening, Nell heard the door open and close. She felt Sir Charles's nearness as he came to stand directly behind her.

"Have you been happy, Nell?" The softness of his voice took her by surprise.

Her mouth went dry, her pulse began racing wildly. It was as if the past three years had never been and she was once again his darling Nell, with his diamond on her finger to prove it. Her head was bent, and she felt his warm breath stirring the wisps of hair on her neck. Opening her eyes, Nell was brought rapidly back to reality by the sight of her naked ring finger.

In a voice not quite steady, she answered, "Of course I have. The school has become quite established, you know. We even have a waiting list for boarders next year," she added with a touch of pride.

"You have taxed yourself too much," he commented in that low, stroking tone. "You are far too thin, too pale, Nell. You've exhausted yourself needlessly—"

"Of course I have not," she protested with the merest quaver in her voice. "Now that the school is becoming known, I—I scarcely seem to work at all."

The heat of his breath upon her neck increased, and a shiver coursed the length of her spine as his warm lips pressed into the softness of her neck. She let the delight of it overwhelm her for one brief, delicious moment. Then pride rescued her. Whirling suddenly, Nell raised her open palm to slap what she knew must be mockery from his face.

He easily trapped her hand in his inexorable grip. For a fleeting instant she was nonplused to discover no trace of the expected mockery on the harsh face inches from her own.

"Oh, Nell, Nell," he whispered hoarsely.

Her eyes closed as his finger lightly traced the line of her delicate cheek beside her defiant, upturned nose. He drew her against him and, as if possessing a will of its own, her head tilted back to meet his kiss. Her lips parted, she tasted his breath. Then suddenly she was jolted by his release.

Springing open, her eyes took in his sneering lips, his jeering blue eyes. Standing like stone, trying to assimilate the meaning of what had happened, trying simply to recall how to breathe, Nell stared at him. His square face, with strength of purpose in every line, his heavy black brows and thick, curling mass of black hair—all these were as she had remembered them. But the cynical lift of his lips and the derisive glint in his eyes were entirely different from the tender, passionate expression she remembered so well. New, too, was the caustic tone of his voice.

"I congratulate you on your success," he was saying. "I'm certain being instructress to so many children must be far more gratifying than being mother to a few."

She gasped at his audacity. Then she regained control and said crushingly, "Teaching children is certainly preferable to the prospect of mothering *yours!*"

At first she feared he would strike her. He raised his hand in a menacing manner, and his eyes went murderously dark. But with amazing self-control, he lowered his hand to flick an invisible speck from the sleeve of his bottle-green coat. The rhythmic flexing of his cheek remained the only sign of his intense anger as he moved to stand near the pedimented window overlooking the street below.

As if from a great distance, Nell studied the tension in his erect stance. Shock and annoyance engulfed her as she silently berated herself for responding so wantonly to his touch. She had wanted his kiss, yearned for the caress of his lips upon hers, and this knowledge filled her with bitter shame. He had meant to deliberately disconcert her, of that she was certain, and she cursed her folly at letting him succeed so easily.

How could she, how could she? Nell demanded of herself. How could she still tingle with indefinable stirrings in the presence of this man? No one knew better than she how capable he was of inflicting pain and heartache. She must not allow him to make Beth suffer as she had suffered, as she was still suffering.

Nearly cringing from the tangible hostility in the room, Beth entered, stammering that Fowles would have tea sent up shortly. She made a few awkward attempts at conversation, then fell silent as neither her sister nor her fiancé seemed inclined toward discourse.

At length, tea having been served, Nell inquired of her sister, "When shall you make public the announcement, Beth?"

"I—I don't know," the unhappy girl stuttered.

"I shall insert the notice the day following our engagement ball," said Sir Charles, glaring significantly at Eleanor over the rim of his teacup.

"Oh, are you to have a ball, Beth?" Nell asked pointedly. "Mother made no mention of it in her letter."

"That must be because I have only just decided upon one," explained Sir Charles.

"Do you think, Beth dearest," Nell prodded, "that this is a wise idea? You know how the expense of a ball mounts up, and Papa may not feel sufficiently able to meet the costs."

"Oh, I—I—" Beth began, flustered.

"I shall be taking care of the expenses, my sweet," Sir Charles told his fiancée, "and so you may inform your parents."

"But that's outrageous!" Nell exclaimed, looking directly at him at last. His triumphant smile increased her anger with herself for allowing him to provoke her. She immediately turned her attention back to her sister. "Beth, perhaps you could explain to your fiancé just what people will say when they learn that it is *he* who is giving a betrothment ball for you and not Papa."

"B-but Nell," Beth protested miserably, darting her eyes between the two combatants, "you know Papa said he would never again hold another such ball after you stormed out in the midst of yours!"

Clearly amused, Grayson watched as Eleanor's mouth worked soundlessly. Finally he intervened. "All of this can be arranged at a later time. It was a pleasure to see you again, *sister* dear." He set down his cup with a clatter, ignoring her furious look, and stood up. "Until later, my love," he murmured easily to Beth. Then he was gone.

Unable to move, Nell sat seething for fully two minutes after the door had closed. Then she burst from her chair with volcanic fury.

"How dare he! How dare he come back into my life when I'd just settled quite nicely! You must see that you cannot possibly marry him!" she added as an afterthought to her sister.

"I—I think I must marry him," Beth said mournfully. "It wouldn't be quite the thing for another one of us to jilt him, would it?"

Which effectively stopped Nell in her tracks.

# - 2 -

THAT EVENING THE uproar resulting from the abrupt arrival of their eldest daughter led to the cancellation of Mrs. Trant's plans to attend the opera and drove Mr. Trant to his club at an unconscionably early hour. Horace Trant's desertion left the battlefield solely to his wife, Eugenia, who seemed more than prepared to meet the severe accusations which fell steadily from Eleanor's pretty lips.

Whether she pleaded, badgered, or raged, Nell's opposition to the improper betrothment of her younger sister to Sir Charles Grayson had not the least effect on her mother's implacable belief that the match could not be more ideal.

"Really, child, I do not perfectly understand you," Mrs. Trant declared wearily, fanning herself listlessly as she sat too near the fire in her boudoir. "Surely you cannot wish every member of the family to remain a spinster?"

Mentally counting to ten, Nell responded as calmly as she could after several hours of argumentation with her esteemed parent. "Of course not, Mama. But I do not like to see Beth thrown as a sacrificial lamb to such a domineering, licentious man as Grayson."

"Come now, Eleanor," her mother reproved. "You are merely worried that people will look upon you as the jilt, is that not it? But I do not think you should let any considerations of your own past folly overshadow Elizabeth's good fortune."

"You mean the family's good fortune!" Nell flared disrespectfully.

"I cannot deny that your father has made certain ... unhappy ... decisions recently and that Sir Charles has kindly offered to remove the consequences of those decisions from our lives," her mother agreed placidly. She folded her fan and pronounced her desire not to continue this discussion. "If Elizabeth did not wish to marry Sir Charles, it would be another matter altogether, but as she has been most willing to go ahead with this marriage, I cannot think what opposition you can possibly have."

"Very well, Mama," Nell relented with a frustrated sigh. Arguing with her indolent but indomitable mother had always been fruitless. Tonight it left Nell with a headache, and she gave in with ill grace. "If I cannot make you and Papa see that Beth should not marry where she does not love—"

"Many times arranged marriages are the happiest, Eleanor," her mother interrupted, rising with a swish of her ruffled peignoir. "With time Beth may well grow to love her husband."

"Better she should love a snake!"

"To listen to you, one would think you are jealous of your sister's alliance." Mrs. Trant glanced shrewdly at her daughter as she drifted out of the room, her lace ruffle trailing behind her full figure like the wake behind a sailing ship.

She left Nell rooted to the floor, staring in horror at her mother's receding form. Jealous! That was absurd, utterly and completely absurd! She did not love Sir Charles. If she deigned to feel anything about him at all, it was quite a different emotion. Wasn't it? Shivering, she almost felt again his finger tracing the line of her cheek, felt his breath tantalizing her lips, which had been eager for his kiss. She burned with renewed shame as she recalled the scene that afternoon. Her mother called drowsily out to her.

"Yes, Mama?" she asked dully.

"How long will you be staying, Eleanor? If you would like to make yourself useful," she went on without waiting for a reply, "there are many, many arrangements to be made, especially now that Sir Charles has decided he would like to hold a ball in Elizabeth's honor. I do not see how I can possibly manage it all."

Nell nearly laughed aloud. It was as if everything she had been saying were no more than the merest wisp of her imagination. Not one word had made the least impression on her mother! And now her mother appeared perfectly willing to turn over the chore of planning the wedding to the groom's former fiancée.

But then, Nell had known how it would be before she stepped into the coach in Norwich, the capital city of Norfolk. Beth, bending like a willow to the strongest breeze; Mama, immovable in her own dilatory way; Papa, hiding in his club whenever greeted with the least unpleasantness. She had known it would be this way, known her coming would be useless. So why *had* she come to London? It was, Nell feared, a question she did not want to answer.

Rubbing her temples, she retired to her own room, which had been hers before her departure to Norfolk to open the Establishment for Young Ladies with her old school friend, Drusilla Poole. Little had been changed, and somehow Nell found that comforting. The old bed still sagged in the middle and the floorboard at the side still creaked when stepped on. Silly, but she would miss that when she returned to her neat, impersonal room at the school. Which, of course, she must do without delay.

She reclined upon the high, narrow bed and stared at the familiar faded pattern on the flowered paper walls, one arm thrust in a graceful arc over her throbbing head. Mama was wrong, she told herself. She was not jealous. The love she had once felt for Sir Charles had died long ago. If the other, more elemental yearnings had not yet been conquered, she must simply learn to ignore them.

Confronting the painful truth, she admitted that seeing Sir Charles, even so briefly, had stoked anew the lingering embers of her desire for him. It grieved Nell deeply to acknowledge her heated response to his attractive masculinity, and she knew she must smother the flame before it burst out of control.

With a heavy sigh, she snuffed the candle flame, then

tossed fitfully in the darkness. How could she let him destroy Beth, as he surely would with his temper and his overbearing ways? Mournfully she reminded herself that she had nothing to say to the matter and eventually fell asleep with a frown still creasing her brow.

In the morning, however, Nell's headache had quite gone, and everything appeared in a sharper focus with the early sunlight. Even the floorboard did not make a sound when she rose from her bed. Within the hour she was seated in the morning room at the drop-down desk of an old, battered secretary, writing an explanation to Miss Poole. She would be staying on, she wrote her friend, for a short, indefinite period of time to help with wedding preparations. It was fortunate, was it not, that the end of the school term was nearing and she could so easily be spared for a few brief weeks?

Having folded and sealed her missive, Nell smoothed the front of her muslin round gown, straightened the long, plain sleeves, and set off in search of her family to impart to them the joyful news that she meant to remain. With the exception of her mother, who always breakfasted in bed and never earlier than noon, she found her family members around the oval table in the sunny breakfast room. Papa was sipping coffee—no doubt laced with spirits—and Beth was daintily sinking her small, even teeth into a slice of honeyed bread. Nell poured herself a cup of tea and announced that she would be staying on in London for a bit.

"Excellent! Excellent!" puffed her father in his gruff way.

"I'm glad you think so, Papa," Nell said demurely, closely watching her sister.

Beth's face had ever mirrored her emotions. Relief and gratitude now crossed the pliant features in full measure, but in addition to these feelings Nell saw—what? Apprehension? Nell wondered if Beth was afraid that she would quarrel with Sir Charles again. She knew yesterday's confrontation had greatly overset her younger sister. Beth had never been able to abide the least argument.

"And I swear, dearest Beth, I shall be on my best behavior for my entire stay!" Nell promised with a laugh, stretching out her hand to cover her sister's. "Not one word of reproach shall pass my lips with regard to Sir Charles!"

\* \* \*

Her resolution vanished within ten minutes of the baronet's arrival that afternoon to drive Beth through the Park. Nell greeted him pleasantly enough, though she watched him warily. Certainly, she could not fault Sir Charles on the cut or style of his clothes. But then he had always patronized the finest tailors, and he wore the tight buff breeches and long-tailed burgundy coat with the unconcerned air of one who has purchased the best.

Hooded by half-lowered lids in a manner that caused Nell's breath to catch in her throat, his sapphire eyes openly inspected every inch of her slim figure as he expressed his delight that she would be staying on in Mount Street. In a voice heavy with concern, he then inquired, "But you do not think Trant's Establishment for Young Ladies will collapse in your absence, do you?"

She focused her eyes on the intricate folds of his ivory silk cravat and answered sweetly, "I trust you find your own wit pleasing, sir, for I assure you no one else does."

She looked up to find his deep blue eyes now shimmering with ill-placed humor and she quickly lowered her gaze to the ruffled edge of her own primrose gown. She told her sputtering heart to cease being nonsensical and get back to the business of beating regularly. Instead it began beating even more rapidly at the look accompanying Sir Charles's placid response.

"My own wit pleases me well enough," he said politely. "May I add, dear sister-to-be, that your ill humor does not become you."

The mild tone drew an annihilating stare from Nell, and her heart-shaped lips parted, intending to inform Sir Charles that his opinion of what became her was a matter of the veriest indifference to her. But, catching sight of Beth's blanched features, Nell forced herself to be content with turning her lips up into a chilly smile.

Beth's obvious relief smote Nell's conscience. Renewing her effort to maintain a friendly appearance with Sir Charles, she indicated a chair. "If you would take a seat, sir, whilst Beth fetches her bonnet?"

The properly gracious accents, complete with welcoming gesture, brought a low laugh from the gentleman. "A lesson in etiquette, Miss Trant?" he teased, flashing a charming, off-center smile.

Beth fluttered between them. "I shall only be the merest moment, Sir Charles," she said quickly, then continued to hang quivering in mid-step as if she were afraid to leave them alone together.

Nell's mother, floating gracefully into the room, rescued Beth. Mrs. Trant skimmed languorously toward them, the fringe of her drooping shawl dusting the floor behind her plump figure.

"Are you ready, Beth, dear?" she asked sleepily, scanning them all through heavy-lidded, sparkling eyes.

"Ready, Mama?" repeated the bewildered Elizabeth.

"How silly of me, to be sure," her mother replied, sinking like a setting sun onto the sofa cushions. "Did I not tell you we must go to Madame Despois for a fitting?"

"A fitting?" Beth echoed.

"Child, child." Eugenia sighed wearily. "For a ball gown, naturally. You must, of course, have a new gown for the announcement of your betrothal."

Sir Charles looked up from contemplating his well-manicured nails to address Eugenia Trant directly. "But I have called to take Miss Elizabeth for a drive through the Park."

"If you wish to go for a drive," Eugenia said, yawning, "take Eleanor. She could use the fresh air to put some color in her cheeks. I must exert myself now on behalf of my youngest." With that she rose valiantly and drew Beth like a leaf in a gentle breeze out the door.

"Well?" Sir Charles inquired, raising one black brow.

"Well what?" Nell returned on a waspish note. Being abruptly alone with him disturbed her more than she would ever admit.

"Would you care to accompany me for a drive through the Park?" he asked patiently, standing with athletic grace but remaining at a distance from her.

How could he be so casual after all they had shared in the past? she wondered with a spurt of anger. Each time she saw him she wanted to run him through with a sword. The violence of her emotions had frightened her and loosened the already too-slack rein on her ungovernable temper, and she knew better than to expose herself to the dangers of remaining alone with him.

"Well?" he prodded.

"Yes," she replied tersely, "I'll be but a moment."

Nell strode from the room, dismayed at having agreed when she had clearly intended to decline. But having committed herself to accompanying him, she meant to surprise Sir Charles with her amicability. Thus, having added one plumed bonnet and one spangled shawl to her attire, she was smiling prettily as he led her outside. Nevertheless, she paused when she caught first sight of the sporty carriage.

"But where is your groom?" she asked, eyeing with disfavor the light, two-wheeled cab chaise.

Handing her up into her seat, Grayson climbed up beside her and collected the reins before answering. "Use that pretty head of yours, Miss Trant," he said easily. "Where would he sit?"

She had to admit there was scarcely room for the two of them, much less a groom. All too aware of the closeness of Sir Charles's muscular buckskin-clad thigh, Nell felt a perverse need to give him a set-down.

"You intended to take Beth out without a groom?" A speaking look companioned her disapproving tone.

"We are affianced, remember," he commented without so much as a glance in her direction.

"That is no excuse for exposing Beth to malicious talk!"

"It is fortunate, then, is it not," Sir Charles pointed out evenly, "that I am driving you instead?"

Nell sputtered with indignation, but recalled her intent to remain outwardly friendly and thus refrained from making a heated rejoinder. Grayson expertly guided his horse, a large, powerful bay, through the noisy, crowded streets, and Nell fell to silently remonstrating with herself. Ignoring the colorful animation of London traffic, she scolded herself for losing her temper—again!—with her all-too-provoking escort. If she were going to extract Beth from this improper betrothment—and she most assuredly desired to!—then she must guard her tongue with the baronet, no matter how great the provocation.

Following upon this resolution, she waited patiently as Grayson pulled onto the less crowded path of the Park and slowed. The fashionable hour had not yet begun and few riders or carriages moved to distract their attention. Nell smiled at Sir Charles and remarked quite warmly, "That was well done! You have quite the lightest hands of anyone I know."

"Such praise, Miss Trant, nearly unmans me," he answered mockingly.

"I meant to be civil," she retorted before she could stop herself, "but it's obviously a grace you have yet to acquire."

"But, my dear, you must excuse me on the grounds that I have not been led to expect civility from you."

Nell sat rigidly erect, fighting to control her temper. His soft, teasing laughter brought her flashing eyes around to cross with his. Woven into the cynical amusement of his dark gaze was an intensity of emotion that robbed Nell of words as she stared, unable to decipher the message she saw. The fire died out of her green eyes, and she lowered her red-gold lashes to hide her secrets.

"Like dog and cat," Eleanor sighed. "That's how we are together."

After an imperceptible pause, Sir Charles said gently, "There was a time, Nell—"

"Over and done with," she hastily put in.

"Over and done with," he agreed dryly.

Copper curls swept over her cheek as Nell turned away. Why must he bring up the past? The past had been so safely encased in a numb, not-to-be-touched part of her. Releasing it now only pierced her more sharply than before. She could not bear it if he actually became a member of her family. To see him often would be unendurable!

The cab chaise slowed further still, then stopped moving altogether. Still Nell did not look up, keeping her head averted to avoid the hurt awaiting her when she gazed into his mocking eyes. A finger lightly flicked her cheek. Startled, she turned to meet his scrutiny. The harsh cynicism had vanished; the severe lines had all smoothed from his squared jaw. A dark glimmer reflected like sunlight on rippling water within his sapphire eyes and streaks of blue highlighted his dark curls as he tilted his head to study her.

"There were times when we did not always argue," he murmured huskily. His hand cupped her chin, his thumb gently stroking the curve of her cheek. "You remember them, Nell, I know you do."

Each breath dragged through her like a hot coal, burning and tearing her throat. However much her treacherous body longed to be enfolded within the remembered muscular contours of his, Nell feverishly denied such desires. Painful memories of their last, devastating argument quickly smothered the flame his touch ignited.

Pulling her head from his light grasp, she said coldly, "Of course we didn't always argue. But I'm certain Alicia—or was it Venetia?—remembers such times far better than I."

His hand dropped to his side, the mockery returned to his eyes, and Sir Charles matched her tone as he responded, "I couldn't say. It has been some time since Alicia."

"Oh, I'm certain you haven't lacked for companionship," Nell retorted heatedly. "Just how many successors has she had in the last three years?"

"I am afraid I have not kept count, my dear," Sir Charles answered evenly.

Watching the flexing muscles of his jaw, Nell knew he was very angry indeed, and she realized with a guilty start that she had prompted another quarrel. But, said a tiny voice within her, far better to argue with Sir Charles than to yield to his overwhelming attraction.

"Once you have married Beth do you intend," she asked tartly, "to continue your charming habit of parading your light skirts before all of London?"

"That, my dear, is none of your concern," he replied, tight-lipped.

"Oh, but Beth is very much my concern, Sir Charles!" Nell snapped. "And I, for one, do not intend to stand back and watch you humiliate her before the eyes of the *ton* with your unscrupulous antics."

"Odd that *you* should lecture on the subject of humiliating public behavior, Miss Trant," Sir Charles flared, thoroughly angry at last. "What you put me through at our very public betrothment ball—"

"Was only what you deserved!" Nell cut in furiously.

Glaring at each other, they sat locked in hostile silence. Nell clearly remembered the bitter moment three years before, when their engagement had ended within the colorful glitter of a crowded ballroom. A vision arose of herself remaining stiff and unresponsive as Sir Charles gathered her into his arms for the solitary waltz that was in their honor.

"What is it, my darling Nell?" he had queried after once

swirling the length of the room without words. "You seem oddly out of sorts for what should be a most joyous occasion."

"Nothing," Nell returned in a hollow voice, keeping her eyes fixed steadfastly on a point beyond his shoulder.

"Don't talk such fustian," Sir Charles gently chided, his eyes searching the curves of her face. His hand tensed upon her slim waist, but he continued to smile as they whirled together. "I know you too well to be taken in by such nonsense. Something has overset you, my love, and I wish to know what."

The words, though calmly spoken, were underscored by a tone of command. At last Nell raised her eyes to meet his. In a suffocated voice, she explained, "I have learned that you have resumed relations with Alicia Alverton." She thought her heart would break simply to utter the words. Desperately, she wanted him to deny it, to put her fears to rest.

"Don't be a little fool," he had said sharply.

Her heart had begged her to stop, to let it rest at that, but her pride reared up, overshadowing all else. "You do think me a fool, don't you, Sir Charles?" she said disdainfully. "Well, I am not such a goose as to tamely accept your mistress! You thought to keep her discreetly out of sight, perhaps until after the wedding, but Miss Poole informed me of your meeting with her today—*today* of all days!" she finished contemptuously.

"Miss Poole is an interfering, caper-witted spinster," Sir Charles stated unequivocably. "If you had the least sense—"

"If I had the least sense," Nell interrupted heatedly, "I would never have allowed myself to become entangled with a man of your stamp!"

"And precisely what, may I inquire, do you mean by that?" he asked icily. His fingers curled tightly around her slender hand in a crushing grip.

"I take leave to tell you, sir, that I will not countenance your succession of lady-loves during our marriage!" she snapped in a harsh whisper.

A deep red flush slowly stained his square cheeks, signaling his suppressed anger. "What you do or do not countenance, my love," Sir Charles returned in a tightly controlled tone, "is not of the least importance. And my affairs most certainly do not concern Miss Drusilla Poole!"

Eleanor's slippered foot faltered and they stopped, standing immobile in the center of the marble floor, surrounded by hundreds of well-wishers. As Sir Charles made to regain his hold upon her waist, Nell's hurt found expression at last.

"Thank you!" she said in a clear, cold voice that carried over the dwindling strains of music. "I was under the misapprehension that my wishes would be of some importance to you! Thank you for having the goodness to open my eyes!"

"Nell, for God's sake," he began on a hoarse undertone.

"I would not dream of being a meddlesome wife," she continued loudly, impervious to the stunned silence now surrounding them. "In point of fact, I wouldn't dream of being your wife at all!"

She slid the ring from her finger and sent it clattering to the polished marble floor with the resounding finality of a death knell. Then, before anyone could react, she turned and fled from the ballroom, her skirt billowing in a blur of ivory. As a babble began to rise like a distant thunder, the very tall, very plain figure of Miss Drusilla Poole separated from the ranks of highly interested spectators to follow Nell's vanishing form.

It had indeed been a very public humiliation, and even the merest memory of it still pierced Nell's heart. The power of Sir Charles Grayson to cause her such great pain had not dimmed. She felt it now as deeply as she had felt it then. Remembering it all, their proximity in the small cabriolet adding to her discomfiture, Nell realized that, if anything had been needed to convince her of the dire necessity to end Beth's betrothment, this drive had been it.

Obviously he had not changed, unless he had grown more profligate. Certainly, he did not care enough for Beth to alter his rakish ways, even as he had not cared enough for Nell to do so. Nell's nebulous desire to save her young sister from her own folly crystalized into solid determination.

Sir Charles was the first to recover. With a fierce snap of the reins, he set his horse going at a frighteningly fast pace. They exchanged not one word during the swift drive back to Mount Street, but the air between them spoke volumes. As soon as he halted before her town home, Nell climbed down. "I do not need your help, thank you!" she said curtly.

As she sped up the steps, she heard him drive away and could not help turning to watch the tall, proud back disappear from view.

# - 3 -

DUST MOTES DANCED in the shaft of morning light spilling across the lowered desktop of the cherrywood secretary. Nell laid down the quill and raised her arms in a long stretch above her head, trying to ease the ache from her shoulders. She felt weary and her hand was cramping, but she still had a sizable stack of invitations to address. A sigh escaped her as she brought her arms down to lean against the scarred wood of the desk. Mama, of course, had not had the energy to help with the invitations to Beth's ball, and her young sister's few efforts had been hopelessly smudged, so the task had fallen, as she had known it would, to Nell.

The tight, high-collared bodice of her pine-green dress heaved as Nell sighed again. Why was she still in London? she asked in momentary frustration. Her attempts during the past week to bring Beth to her senses had been, she must admit, singularly unsuccessful. The realization had slowly come upon her that Beth did not care about Sir Charles Grayson's unsuitability as a husband simply because she did not care in the least about Sir Charles himself. Further, the baronet was all that was kind and considerate toward her sister, making him seem entirely suitable to Elizabeth.

Sir Charles. As always, the thought of him clouded Nell's reflection, and her slim figure tensed. Throughout the week

23

Sir Charles and she had behaved toward one another like distant acquaintances—with a polite, but unfeeling graciousness. Watching the dust waltz through the air, Nell wondered for the thousandth time why he had spoken and touched her so gently upon her first arrival, why he had not again repeated the warm intimacy. Obviously he had expected to smooth everything over with his usual charm. But she was no longer a young miss ready to be beguiled by a handsome face and a pretty manner! She knew full well how shallow the baronet's charm was, and she knew better than to fall under its spell.

Crossing her arms, Nell ran her hands down the long, narrow sleeves that descended from a puff at the shoulders of her gown. Without knowing why, she felt chilled. If she were to be painfully honest, she could not deny the power of Sir Charles's charm, or her own secret disappointment at not being the continued recipient of his attention. She wondered again why she was lingering in London. Reacquaintance with Sir Charles had proved to be thoroughly unsettling. She had even felt, she was forced to ruefully acknowledge, an undeniable hostility toward Beth—sweet, inoffensive Beth!—each time Sir Charles had called upon her sister this week.

With an impatient shake of her head that sent her copper ringlets escaping from the confines of a white satin ribbon, Nell shoved all such thoughts from her mind. She was in no mood for such self-recriminations. Collecting her pen with vigor, she dipped it into the squat ink-stand and began again to address envelopes with her neat, flowing script. Her concentration was so intense that when a soft voice from behind her asked, "Working hard, Nell?" her hand jerked convulsively, knocking over the inkpot and spilling ink all over the desk.

"Oh! Look what you made me do!" she cried as she leapt to her feet and frantically pulled envelopes clear of the inky flow. "What did you mean by sneaking up on me?" she demanded.

"Allow me—" Sir Charles began.

"Haven't you done enough?" Nell snapped.

"Move out of the way, you little fool!" he ordered curtly. Forcibly pushing her to one side, Sir Charles began mopping up the black flow with brisk, thorough swipes of a large square of monogrammed linen.

Her breath coming in short, angry gasps, Eleanor stood watching him in fury. He had no right to walk in unannounced, oversetting her in such a manner! Indignantly, she eyed the back of his well-cut snuff-brown coat and studied the snug fit of his fawn pantaloons. He was nothing but a dandy, and the sudden pounding of her pulses had nothing to do with the studied disarray of his thick black curls or the breadth of his shoulders beneath that superfine coat. It had to do with the ill-bred manner in which he had startled her!

"Are you accustomed to treating all houses as if you own them?" Nell asked with heavy sarcasm, her fingers curling tightly around the vellum envelopes in her hands.

"Had I realized you were within, my dear, I would surely have knocked, if only to please you," he answered calmly without looking at her.

Nell's fingers clenched the vellum rigidly. "Whether or not you thought I was here, you should have knocked."

"Is this your school lesson on etiquette, Miss Trant?" Sir Charles inquired with interest. He cast a glance over his shoulder in time to catch the stormy glare Nell threw at him.

"Why do you never," she asked through clenched teeth, "show Beth this face of yours? With *her* you are all that is amiable. I fear you mislead her greatly as to your true nature."

Sir Charles slowly turned to face her. His heavy lids dropped over his azure eyes, hiding their expression. The only sign of his annoyance was the muscle flexing in his square jaw. Silence stretched between them until Nell thought she could no longer bear it. Her gaze fastened on the worn pattern of the carpet, and she told herself she hated him, hated him.

"Miss Elizabeth," drawled the baronet at last, "has far too much wisdom to provoke me. *That* is a lesson for you to learn."

Her eyes shot upward to his handsome face, and her body shook with wordless outrage. How dare he put the blame for his ill temper on her! He was quite the rudest, the most arrogant, the worst—

"Come, I am sorry I disturbed you, Nell," he said in a conciliatory tone. "It was not my intention, I assure you. I came only to discover what help you may require in preparing for the ball."

"I need none of your help," Nell stated stubbornly.

But her protective anger was already dissipating. How could she maintain her temper when *he* did not? He was the most disobliging creature alive, and Beth was welcome to him! She would not, Nell reminded herself resolutely, allow him to continue to affect her irrational, contrary senses. She only wished he would not look at her in quite that way . . .

Looking away from his disturbing gaze, she focused on the sodden linen still hanging in his hand, black ink bleeding into the delicate material from lace edge to lace edge.

"You've ruined your handerchief," Nell observed flatly.

"It doesn't matter." He tossed the spoiled cloth onto the desk behind him, Nell's eyes following the movement.

"Of course it matters," she contradicted. With three quick steps her long, dark green skirt flaring slightly, Nell joined him at the desk. Dropping the envelopes beside the linen, she asked in a tight little voice, "How much?"

"My dear—"

"How much?" she clipped again.

"Fifty pounds the dozen," he replied shortly.

"Fifty pounds!" she gasped, her eyes wide with shock. Quickly recovering, she brushed past his tall form, forcing herself to remain calm as her arm lightly grazed his. With a sharp jerk she pulled open one of the desk drawers. "That would be four pounds, three shillings, fourpence each," she recited like a shopkeeper counting change.

Nell's hand closed over several coins in the drawer, but as she withdrew them she heard a hiss of breath behind her. In one swift, hostile motion, Grayson trapped her. His gloved hand came down forcefully over hers, clamping the coins beneath it to the top of the desk. His muscular body pinned her slim form against the wood, which cut painfully into her back.

"What the devil do you think you are doing?" he demanded in a voice of barely controlled fury.

"I shall, of course, pay you for the handkerchief," Nell managed to reply steadily, though her breath came fitfully.

His heavy black brows nearly met at the center, and his lips curled upward. His body was pressed so closely upon hers that Nell could feel his muscles tense with anger. Her heart faltered in its beat, and she trembled as she felt his breath lash against her cheek.

"Despise me if you must, Nell," he rasped, "but don't insult me."

A riot of red suffused her features, marking her instant remorse. She wondered if she had indeed seen that flash of hurt cross through his dark eyes. She could not hold his accusing gaze. Her lashes dropped to the curve of her flushed cheeks.

"Of course I don't despise you," she said in a muffled voice.

"Don't you?" mocked Sir Charles.

"Of course not!" Her stain of guilt deepened. He was so near that she could hear him breathe and feel the ripple of his muscles before he stepped away. She strove to bring her own ragged breathing under control as she watched him from behind the thick fringe of her lashes.

Moving to the center of the room, he pulled off his York tan gloves and stood snapping them together, his face expressionless. With sudden surprise, it came to Nell that Sir Charles did not believe her. Though his eyes were again hidden by his lowered lids, she could see the disbelief in every line of his inflexible stance, in the restless click of the leather gloves. Though she did not pause to question why, the thought pained her, and she knew she must not permit such a mistaken belief to continue.

She took a step forward, raised a placating hand. "Forgive me!" she begged with a tremulous smile. "I have been unbearably rude. It's my ungovernable temper. When the ink spilt, I'm afraid so did my humor."

He studied her face before responding in a voice without inflection, "There is nothing to forgive. My own temper was as much at fault as yours."

With a restless movement, he wandered over to stand before the small fire in the grate, then slapped his gloves upon the white mantel. After a lengthy pause, he shot a penetrating look at her over his shoulder and said with a rueful twist of his lips, "Can we not agree, my dear, to meet without coming to blows? If you are to lay me out in lavender each time we meet, I very much fear we shall not get through this betrothment of mine."

Nell tried desperately to stifle a stab of pain. "Naturally, we can agree," she said as evenly as she could. "Let us put all thoughts of the past behind us, Sir Charles, for Beth's sake as much as our own."

"For all our sakes, then," he agreed. He took another turn about the room before stating casually, "Your mother has informed me that you are handling all the preparations for the ball, and for the wedding. I thought, perhaps, if you required help in any way—"

"No, no," Nell cut in hastily. "There is no need, Sir Charles. I have everything well in hand, I assure you."

He ran his deep blue gaze over the haphazard pile of vellum envelopes on the desk. "You were addressing all those on your own?"

"Yes."

"My housekeeper could assist you in such matters," he started, only to be silenced by the abrupt flutter of her hands.

"I can only repeat, Sir Charles, that there is no need. It is quite enough that you are standing the nonsense for everything from the hiring of Gunter's to the settlement with Madame Despois. You must allow us to manage the rest."

"You mean, allow *you* to manage it, my dear," he chided softly. "And you speak of my conceited pride."

"It is not pride!" she denied, stiffening beneath the darkling glitter of his eyes. "You must see how it would look should we simply allow you to handle the reins of this affair."

He stared at her for a long moment, then surprised her by throwing back his dark head to laugh. "Oh, Nell, Nell," he said through his deep laughter, "if you have ever let anyone have the handling of your ribbons, it is the greatest piece of news to me!"

Gradually the stiff lines of her mouth relaxed and she joined him in genuine laughter. Still Nell felt a twinge of conscience. Her nature *had* become too unbending, too implacable! As they grew calm, she determined to disprove his poor opinion of her and set about it by briskly summoning tea, then graciously bidding him to take a seat.

Grayson dragged an armless chair from a shadowy corner

designed to hide its patched cushion and set it beside hers at the secretary. "Allow me to go over the guest list with you," he said with a smile. "I have, in fact, brought a small list of obscure relatives my mother recollected we possessed and thus, of course, must not again be forgotten."

His smile was engaging, his manner even more so. When he chose to be, Sir Charles could be irresistible, as Nell knew only too well. As she took the chair positioned so disturbingly close to his, she inquired after the health of Lady Grayson, a small, energetic and entirely captivating woman for whom Nell still felt a deep affection.

The tea arrived as the baronet was answering cheerfully that his mother was as much of a whirlwind as ever. Fowles departed after serving them, and they set to work poring over the neatly compiled list of names. They had not progressed far before Sir Charles reminded Nell of a mutual acquaintance whose habit of inhaling his snuff too deeply, then sneezing loudly for fully an hour afterwards, had at one time been a shared jest between them. Their tea sat forgotten as the morning room echoed with comfortable laughter, and it was thus, with his black curls bent close to her bright ringlets, that Beth found them some twenty minutes later.

She burst through the door with an uncharacteristic flurry. "Oh, Nell, I've just been speaking with Mama and—" Catching sight of the two figures bending over the papers on the desk, she halted abruptly midway into the room and stood flushed with confusion.

A flash of irritation raced through Nell, quickly replaced by a flood of guilt. Though she had been enjoying her *tête-à-tête* with Sir Charles, it certainly gave her no right to feel annoyed over an interruption. Particularly over an interruption from his fiancée! Nell covered her guilty start with a beaming smile as she rose from her chair to greet her sister.

"Yes, Beth dearest? What is it?" she prompted, noting the acute distress passing over Beth's round features like clouds over a troubled sky. "You were looking for me, were you not?"

"Yes! No! That is—" Beth stammered in evident agitation.

Puzzlement sketched Nell's brow as she watched her young sister strive for composure. Her bewilderment was mirrored in the baronet's square features as he, too, stood up to greet Beth.

"If you seek to be private with your sister, Miss Beth, I shall be happy to remove myself," he offered kindly, watching her closely.

"No, no," she answered quickly, taking a deep breath and smiling prettily at them both. "I am being silly, I know. I was looking for you, Nell," she admitted, taking a seat upon the frayed sofa. "I have been speaking with Mama about attending Lady Harlowe's ball, but she says she is promised to the Duchess of Cumberleigh's card-party that evening and cannot chaperone me." Beth raised her corn-flower-blue eyes from the knot she had been pleating in the skirt of her king's-blue day dress to fix them pleadingly on her sister's face. "And Mama has said you will not go. But if you do not go, how am I to attend?"

Nell regarded her sister in some surprise. Usually Beth did not care where they went. She was content to follow in their mother's indolent steps, meeting the Society that Mama chose for her. But the look of entreaty in Beth's eyes was clear. She very much cared about going to Lady Harlowe's champagne ball, and Nell did not know how she was going to refuse her.

Refuse her, however, Nell meant to do. She had been firm in her determination not to attend such functions. Although she had told her mother she was too long upon the shelf to enjoy such occasions, Nell knew a part of her could not bear to see Sir Charles and Beth dancing and laughing together while she sat hopelessly removed from such gaiety. Just thinking of it brought an edge to her voice when she responded.

"There are plenty of other parties and balls to attend this Season, Beth. Surely you'll not miss one ball."

"But I will!" countered Elizabeth with rare animation. "You *must* escort me to Lady Harlowe's, Nell, you *must!*"

What start is this? wondered Eleanor as she gazed speculatively at her sister. "I'm sorry, Beth, but you know I do not intend to go about during my stay in Town," she said slowly.

Beth's crestfallen expression gave evidence to her disappointment. Her hands fluttered over her dress once more and she said quietly, "Could you not make an exception this one time? It means a great deal to me."

"But why?" Nell insisted. "Why should this one ball be any different from all the others?"

"Because *he* will be there," Beth replied jerking her head up. As soon as the words left her mouth, scarlet streaked over her usually creamy cheeks, and her hands flew to cover them. "I mean—I mean—"

"I believe, Miss Trant, that Miss Beth is trying to say she has learned that I am engaged to Lady Harlowe for her ball," Sir Charles broke in smoothly. He stepped over to where Beth sat on the sofa and caught the hands hiding her cheeks. "My dear, you have paid me a vast compliment and I am certain that Nell would not wish to spoil it for you." As he spoke he lightly brushed his lips across the backs of her hands, then laid them gently on her lap. He straightened, then turned to stare at Nell with a raised brow. "Would you, Miss Trant?"

"Oh, but I—I did not bring any evening wear with me from Norfolk," she protested weakly. Her nerves felt numb at the sight of that brief tenderness between them. How could she possibly bear an evening filled with such moments? She searched Beth's expressive features. Could she have been wrong? Could it be that Beth did, indeed, carry a secret *tendre* for her fiancé? Nell had not thought it possible, but if Sir Charles's presence at a ball meant so much to her . . .

"We have agreed to have done with arguments, have we not, Miss Trant?" the baronet reminded her gently. "Miss Beth wishes very much to attend this ball, and I would very much appreciate your making it possible for her to do so. Come, I would consider your agreement a gesture of peace-making that would convince me that you do not, in fact, despise me after all."

His wry tone was matched by the twist of his smile. Looking from his harsh, strong features to the receding crimson tide on her sister's delicate face, Nell knew she would give in. But she did so with great reluctance.

"Oh, very well. If it means so much to you, Beth, I will escort you to Lady Harlowe's ball. But," she added, stemming the flow of joyous gratitude she saw on Beth's lips,

"I warn you it is the only ball I mean to be coerced into attending for the duration of my stay, so you had best make the most of it."

"Oh, I shall, I shall!" Beth vowed, jumping up to embrace her sister in a fierce hug. "Thank you, Nell! You are the dearest of sisters! And thank you, Sir Charles, for I am persuaded it was your coaxing, not mine, that produced Nell's agreement."

His deep blue eyes seemed to reflect his rueful acceptance of this praise. His lips curved upward, then spread apart, devastating Nell with one of his most charming off-center smiles. "I shall be awaiting Lady Harlowe's ball with a new anticipation. Miss Trant, Miss Beth," he said with a bow to each before collecting his gloves from the mantel and departing.

Elizabeth danced out behind him, bestowing upon Nell a smile that seemed as nervous as it was apologetic. Nell, however, gave herself over to wishing she could despise Sir Charles Grayson. She, more than anyone, had every reason to! But flying in the face of all logic, Nell found she could not hate him.

# · 4 ·

FOUR NIGHTS LATER, Miss Eleanor Trant sat on the plush velvet of a gilded chair and watched with a smile set firmly on her lips as Sir Charles Grayson entered upon a waltz with her sister Elizabeth. Her eyes followed the motion of the pair across the tiled floor, focusing at first on the triple hem of pleated ruffles that furled against Beth's white silk stockings. Unwillingly Nell's gaze traveled up over the celestial-blue muslin gown to fix on the radiant glow of her sister's face. Beside the soft brown curls of Beth's carefully arranged hair her cheeks glowed a becoming pink, and an intimate smile lifted her full lips. The smile was solely for her partner and, observing it, Nell felt like an intruder.

She forced herself to look away, but within moments her eyes were drawn irresistibly back to Sir Charles. Though most men held themselves stiffly when they danced, the baronet moved with a quick, fluid grace that seemed effortless. Although it had become more and more the fashion for men to wear black evening trousers, with only a few old fogies retaining the style of knee-breeches, Lady Harlowe's view of correct evening wear demanded that men appear at her door looking ready to attend a function at court or to step through the doors of the rigidly exclusive Almack's. And while men whose legs were spindly or bowed might decry Lady Harlowe's demands, Sir Charles certainly had no cause to do so.

White embroidered stockings and black satin breeches accentuated the athletic shape of his long, muscular legs.

A sapphire velvet coat emphasized not only the breadth of his shoulders, but also the intensity of his deep blue eyes. From the top of his carelessly brushed black curls to the tip of his black evening pumps, Sir Charles appeared the quintessence of the *beau ideal*.

As Nell realized the direction of her reflections, she quickly glanced back at her sister and again caught Beth's smile. Nell's hands clenched over the small fan in her lap.

The meaning of that smile was obvious. There could no longer be any doubt, Nell concluded with a wave of melancholy. Beth had succumbed to her fiancé's attractions. Over the past four days, Nell had begun to suspect it, for her sister's eager anticipation of this ball had been quite unlike Beth's usual tranquil acceptance of circumstances about her. During the whole of today, Elizabeth had shone with an inner excitement, her soft blue eyes glinting with unusual brilliance. The opportunity to dance in her beloved's arms, as she was now doing, had given the young miss a pretty animation, and Nell wondered dismally why this fact should cast her into the dismals.

Staring at the copper spangles threaded through the silk of her splayed fan, Nell wished she had not come. Though she knew she did not have the least affection left for Sir Charles, it pained her deeply to watch her sister being gammoned by his all-too-powerful charm.

The faint hiss of nearby whispers attracted her attention. Although she could not hear the content, Eleanor immediately raised her head high. Should anyone gossip about her sister waltzing with her own former fiancé, she, at least, would not add fuel to the malicious flames. Fixing a smile on her lips, she regarded the crush of fashionable people present with all the appearance of one who has never enjoyed herself so much. Bejeweled ladies vied for the favors of dandified swells. Sashes of rose-colored silk festooned the fluted colonnades, as well as the massive curved staircase leading up to it. Champagne flowed freely. Vibrant festivity surrounded Nell, and again she wished she had not come.

Her lips remained curved resolutely upward as the waltz faded, and Sir Charles returned Beth to her side. She dropped her red-gold lashes to hide her eyes as Beth regaled him with gay chatter.

"You should not have refused to waltz with Lord War-wynne, Nell," Beth exclaimed happily as she swirled onto the gilded chair beside her. "It is the most enchanting way in which to circle a room."

"I am certain you would not truly wish for your chaperone to waltz," Nell responded repressingly. "Think how odd it would look."

"If you did not wish to be importuned upon to dance, Miss Trant," Sir Charles drawled, eyeing her slim figure in a most disconcerting fashion, "you should not have worn a gown which becomes you so well."

"How very true!" Elizabeth laughed. "You are looking like a diamond of the first stare tonight, Nell."

Though she had intended at first to wear her drabbest ball gown, complete with one of Mama's turbans, Nell had instead decked herself most becomingly in a cream India muslin gown stitched with metallic copper thread across the bodice and slashed with copper-colored silk in the short, puffed sleeves. A thin ribbon of matching silk defined the high waist, then fell in two enticing strands midway down the front of the flaring cream skirt. The gown was several years old, having originally been purchased as a part of her never-used trousseau, but as she had taken it in to accommodate her thinner figure, Nell had cleverly arranged the skirt to flare slightly more, as was the current fashion.

She fiddled with the ends of the ribbons dangling in her lap, not wanting to acknowledge her reasons for wearing a frock she knew enhanced both the coloring of her hair and complexion to no little degree.

"If the pair of you are trying to turn me up sweet, you are sadly wide of the mark, I assure you!" she said with a small laugh. "You must know that chaperones are by nature resistant to such flattery."

Beth began to protest when several young bucks came to petition both ladies for the country dance forming at that very moment. Nell adamantly refused all invitations, shaking her head until her topknot of curls swayed against the rope of pearls binding it. As she was telling persistent Lord Warwynne that, as she was here in the guise of chaperone, she must again refuse him, Elizabeth broke in upon her with a breathless "Pardon me!"

Turning, Nell saw standing next to Beth a soberly dressed gentleman who was somewhat older than herself, of medium height and build and wearing an air of somber propriety.

"Nell, I should like to present Mr. Josiah Perkins," Beth said in a rush of words. "You may remember seeing him in the Park just after you first arrived."

"Of course," Nell said mendaciously. She did not remember him, but then few people would remember a face that had so little to distinguish it from the ordinary beyond a small cleft in the chin. His brown hair, cropped very short, was not arranged fashionably, and his hazel eyes appeared colorless. He looked utterly respectable and utterly dull. Nell raised her white-gloved hand to his. "How do you do, Mr. Perkins?"

He bent ceremoniously, took her hand, and held it for precisely the proper length of time before releasing it. "I am honored to meet you, Miss Trant," he intoned.

A sparkle of amusement crept into her emerald eyes. What a stiff young man, to be sure.

"May I request the honor of this country dance with Miss Elizabeth Trant?" he asked gravely.

"Certainly, Mr. Perkins," Nell replied, matching his tone. As the pair departed, the corners of her lips twitched, and she only barely smothered a gurgle of laughter. The laugh became a choke, however, as her hands were clasped abruptly and she was pulled lithely to her feet.

"I believe, Miss Trant, it's time we danced." Sir Charles began to lead her firmly toward the set that was forming.

Even this casual contact of his gloved hands on hers produced an unexpected rush of emotion. Her breath caught, and her pulse leapt wildly in response. She dug in the heels of her slim satin slippers and attempted to free her hands from his.

"I don't intend to dance this evening, sir!"

His eyes inspected hers intently for a stretch of time, then with a dazzling smile, he released her. "As you wish, Miss Trant," he said with a half-bow.

She had not expected victory. As her hands fell abruptly to her sides, the sarsenet shawl that was draped from elbow to elbow slid downward. Grasping the thin silk, she ignored her inner disappointment and returned to her chair with as much dignity as she could muster under his mocking gaze.

As she rearranged her shawl over her elbow-length white gloves, Sir Charles disappeared. Nell was nodding her acknowledgment of several women when he reappeared to take the empty chair at her side. The ladies of Nell's acquaintance instantly unfurled their fans, and Nell knew herself to be the object of their gossip. She turned a stormy green gaze upon the source of all her troubles.

"Will you not go away, Sir Charles?" she demanded in a fierce whisper. "People are *talking!*"

"No," he replied easily, handing her a glass of champagne. "You did not wish to dance; therefore I did not wish to dance. And I do not wish to go away."

"But people—"

"People be damned," he interrupted good-naturedly. "They cannot say anything you or I have not heard before, my dear. The devil may fly away with them for all I care."

"Anyone would think you a royal duke," she mumbled into the bubbles of her golden drink.

"And anyone would think you quite the most lovely lady here," he returned caressingly.

Nell's brows shot upward into the soft tendrils of hair falling casually over her brow. She vividly remembered a time when such compliments from his lips had sent her into transports of delight. She was thankful that three years had taught her something. She knew these flattering gems for the imitations they were, given out to every woman of his acquaintance until none had the least value. Sipping from her glass, she watched him over the rim and said nothing.

"Is that not the Dowager Countess of Lampton?" Sir Charles asked after a pause. He lifted his round quizzing glass and peered solemnly through it for some seconds.

Nell followed the direction of his gaze and spied a gleaming vision in purple satin encamped precariously over a saber-legged settee across the room. "Why, yes, I believe it is," she answered with a smile.

Their glances met at the same instant, and they grinned.

"Do you remember the night at Lady Kidwell's when she tipped the punchbowl onto Beau Rundle's lap?" he queried with a light laugh.

"Oh, yes! Or the time at Drury Lane when she fell asleep and snored loudly through the whole of Hamlet's soliloquy?" Nell returned, beginning to giggle.

"I did not think Lampton allowed his mother to go abroad anymore," Sir Charles commented as he raised his glass to inspect the lady in question once more. He dropped his glass, letting it dangle on the end of a finely worked ribbon, then ran his eyes around the room before returning his gaze to Nell's face.

Her heart quickened at the intensity of his steady regard, and her lashes fell to flicker against her delicate cheek. His eyes held something altogether too intimate but though she tried, Nell could not command her tongue to berate him for his audacity.

"And do you remember," Sir Charles said very softly at last, "how it was the night we met, Miss Trant?"

"No," she said quickly, fibbing.

"It was very like this night. Come, you must recall the manner in which we danced," he chided gently.

"No," she repeated stubbornly, shifting in her chair so that only her profile was presented to him. She did not want to remember that night or any other of which he had been a part!

"Perhaps," he continued in a low murmur, "I could help you to recall it . . ."

"And perhaps not!" she retorted, instantly swinging back to him. "You forget yourself, Sir Charles! It is Elizabeth to whom you should be making pretty speeches—"

"Ah," he cut in with a smile of satisfaction.

She eyed him warily for a moment, but could not stop herself from inquiring, "And what do you mean by that?"

"I'm gratified to know, my dear, that you consider recollection of our meeting a 'pretty speech,'" he explained.

Glaring hotly at him for a long second, Nell then tossed off the remnants of her champagne, handed him her empty glass, snapped open her fan, and began briskly waving it before her. Why did she allow him to overset her in this manner? He was as good as betrothed to Beth, yet he was openly flirting with her, flattering her with his ready charm. She did not question his motives. She *knew* him to be nothing but a libertine who no sooner spied a feminine quarry than he must give chase. It was her misfortune that what was mere sport to him was another matter altogether to her!

She caught sight of Beth stepping lightly through the country dance with Mr. Perkins and realized that now, more than ever, she must not allow her fragile, sweet-natured sister be allied to the hard, cynical, licentious Sir Charles. She had not succeeded in making Beth understand his ill-temperament, nor had she convinced Beth that no wife wanted to share a husband with a string of beautiful mistresses. Suddenly Nell thought of a new plan, one that had been forming in her mind for days. If Beth could be brought to see that it was not only Cyprians with whom he dallied...

Nell's captivating India muslin gown had been designed to entice. Peering up at Sir Charles through the curtain of her red-gold lashes, she knew that the gown, at least, had succeeded in its purpose. His blue eyes darkened beneath half-closed lids as they fixed upon the low, square-cut bodice that offered a tantalizing hint of soft, rounded flesh.

Folding her fan, Eleanor faced him, a teasing smile playing upon her lips. "I have been sadly remiss, Sir Charles," she said. "I came to this ball as a gesture meant to establish peace between us, not to foster further ill will."

One black brow climbed, then lowered. His blue eyes regained a shimmer of amusement. "Then say you will dance with me and all will be forgiven, Miss Trant."

"Very well," she agreed demurely, dropping her lashes to hide the triumph in her eyes.

Thus, as soon as Mr. Perkins had returned Beth to her chair, Nell rose to enter the quadrille with Sir Charles, earning herself a fulminating frown from the disgruntled Lord Warwynne.

As their gloved hands came together, Nell's eyes joined with his and she felt her heart skitter, then begin to thump erratically. Surely he must hear it over the music, over the laughter, over the babble of voices filling the room. Unable to withstand the impact of those dark, intense eyes a moment longer, she fixed her own gaze on her feet, pretending to count the steps.

"You dance as delightfully as ever, my dear," Sir Charles commented, forcing her to look up at him.

She pinned a false smile in place and hoped her inner upheaval did not show in her eyes. "Thank you. As I told you before, Sir Charles, you dance with a grace unusual in a man."

His eyes widened slightly, as if he could not believe her unusual amiability. "It has been a great while since you've paid me such a compliment, Nell," he returned caressingly.

Continuing to smile brightly, she began to talk of Edmund Kean's latest brilliant performance at Drury Lane. They had maintained this easy conversation through several turns of the quadrille when Nell's small fan suddenly slipped from her fingers to the floor. As she bent quickly to retrieve it, she surreptitiously loosened the ribbon lacing her satin slipper over her ankle. Straightening, she bestowed an apologetic smile on her partner.

"Forgive me! The cord of my fan somehow gave way," she explained as she took up his hand to resume the dance.

They had managed but a few steps when she faltered over the ribbon of her slipper. "Oh, dear," she said, stopping again to look down at her untied shoe. "I am sorry, Sir Charles. This doesn't appear to be my dance, does it?" She flashed him a coquettish smile of apology, and he quickly took her hand to lead her away from the revolving crowd.

"No matter. 'Tis easily remedied." He guided her into one of a series of secluded alcoves scattered throughout Lady Harlowe's ballroom. It was but a tiny niche with a small seat covered in ice-blue brocade. Nell sat down as Sir Charles yanked the curtained aperture closed. The beat of her heart increased furiously, and her hands shook visibly as she straightened the folds of her skirt. She had sought this *tête-à-tête*, but now that the moment to expose Sir Charles as a hardened womanizer had come, Nell no longer desired to do it. Without seeking to understand her sudden reluctance to remain alone with him, she ran her tongue over dry lips, preparing to tell the baronet to wait for her outside while she retied the laces.

The opportunity, however, was lost as Sir Charles immediately bent down on one knee to capture her small foot in the palm of his hand. His fingers deftly crossed the thin ribbon about her slender ankle, his light touch evoking her unwilling response. She forgot Beth. She forgot the seductive game she had meant to play. She forgot even his previous perfidy. Her senses were betraying her, arousing her with a consuming need. In one last bid for sanity, she started to pull her foot free of his light clasp, but his hand tightened about her ankle, circumventing her escape. The polite words of thanks froze on her lips. For a long moment, neither moved.

"Nell," he whispered thickly at last.

His hand crept upward to the soft curve of her calf, where his fingers stirred restlessly against her silk stocking. She stared down at the glossy black curls bent over her foot and tried to speak out, but could not. Her very breath seemed stilled. A fierce longing to thread her fingers through that thick, dark hair possessed her. Her shaking hand came up, stretched out. Then without warning, before she could realize his intent, Charles bent further still and pressed his lips warmly on her ankle.

"Nell," he murmured again in a near-moan.

He raised his eyes and the dark desire in them made her heart stop beating. With a flash of insight, Nell knew she had wanted this, wanted it from the moment she had first read her mother's letter. But the excitement shuddering through her was too dangerous. She labored to draw each simple breath and knew she must escape before passion overcame sense and she was lost forever.

Suddenly, Sir Charles rose to his feet, his hands reaching out for her. Knowing she must avoid his embrace at all costs, Nell leapt up and attempted to brush past him, but he blocked her way, then stood staring at her with stark longing in his eyes. Looking up the hard line of his body into his darkly flushed face, she shook her head, her coppery tendrils stirring the air between them.

"No!" she breathed.

Her lips parted on the word, and Nell watched his dark eyes rake over her pale face to fasten on them. His gaze bespoke the intensity of his need. Again she tried to push past his broad form, but he gripped her shoulders and gave her a slight shake.

"You can't return yet, you little fool!" he hissed unsteadily.

"No, please," she begged, raising her hand as if to ward him off. She heard his sharp intake of breath, but kept her eyes fixed on the gold curtain beyond his shoulder. She could not again chance meeting the passion in his eyes, for she knew if she did, she could not long withstand it.

"Don't be more of a fool than you can help!" he said harshly. "If you go out looking as you do, without the least hint of color in your cheeks, with your eyes overbright, the tongues *will* begin to clack! Now, if you will resume your seat, and try to calm yourself, I vow I shall not importune upon you any further."

She raised her eyes. A dark stain still covered his taut features and he was breathing heavily. To her surprise, bitterness clouded his eyes as they watched her intently. Slowly, she nodded. His hands fell from her shoulders, and she backed onto the brocade cushion behind her. Twining the copper ribbons of her gown through her fingers, she said in a hollow voice, "Thank you."

When he did not respond, she risked another glance up at him. He was leaning against the frame of the arched doorway, tension in every line of his muscular form. His arms were crossed stiffly over his chest, and he studied the toe of his black evening pump with intense interest. Abruptly, his eyes came up to capture hers, and Nell stifled a small gasp. She could not define what she saw there, but it was not the cynical mockery she had expected.

"You have more color now," he stated flatly. "I think it is safe to return." He held out his arm and numbly, as though from the depths of an indistinct dream, Nell rose to take it. As they moved through the crowded ballroom in silence, she struggled to keep her head high and her smile in place.

While the rest of the room seemed a mere blur, Nell was entirely conscious of the man walking beside her, of his well-toned length and overpowering masculinity. Having proved to herself that Sir Charles was every inch the roué she had known him to be brought her not the least joy, for she knew she could never relate the incident to her sister. Nor would she ever attempt anything like it again. Such games, she had discovered, were much too painful when the player lost.

As they neared the chairs upon which Beth still sat with Mr. Perkins, Nell noted dimly that her sister was bent earnestly toward the rigid young man, her fingers wrapped tightly around the sticks of her closed fan. Nell's slight puzzlement became pronounced as, upon catching sight of their approach, Beth started guiltily. Her round cheeks flamed, and she began speaking brightly of the dreadful squeeze of people to be found spilling through Lady Harlowe's salons.

Nell's bemused gaze traveled to Mr. Perkins, then hardened sharply at the sight of the dull red suffusing his face. His hazel eyes slid away from her own, and her brows rose. She shoved her scattered emotions aside. Something was afoot between the pair, but for once in her life Nell was completely adrift. Why on earth could Beth be looking so conscience-smitten? With characteristic impulsiveness, Nell determined to discover the reason for their guilty flushes.

Grateful for the distraction from her unsettled emotions, she took the seat beside Mr. Perkins. Tapping his knee with her closed fan with a familiarity that made his mouth gape open in surprise, she said with assumed gaiety, "I do trust the pair of you behaved yourselves while we danced." She was rewarded with a fresh mantling of crimson upon Beth's face while Mr. Perkins turned pasty white.

"But of course! I assure you! We merely conversed!" he sputtered in short, quick bursts.

Before Nell could pursue this highly intriguing matter, a foppishly dressed blond youth presented himself before her. "I thought you did not dance tonight, Miss Trant," he said, barely able to disguise the hurt in his voice.

"I am sorry, Lord Warwynne," Nell said quickly. "My sister persuaded me otherwise."

He brightened at this, the scowl leaving his boyish features. "Then you will dance with me?" he asked.

"Oh, but I have promised this dance to Mr. Perkins," Nell said, completely astonishing that gentleman. At his lordship's instant crestfallen look, she added warmly, "But I promise you, my lord, to save the next waltz for you."

Having thus encouraged the youthful viscount, Nell turned with a bright smile to Mr. Perkins and held out her hand. He had no choice but to rise, bow slightly, and take her fingers as she rose gracefully to her feet. Such a want of manners quite obviously shocked the staid Mr. Perkins, and he began dancing with Miss Trant frowning with disapproval. They conversed on neutral topics throughout, Nell gauging the character and worth of the gentleman as they did so. When the music halted, she remained standing.

"Oh, but I should like very much to dance again, Mr. Perkins."

He looked at her aghast. "But it would not do, Miss

Trant! To dance twice in a row! Oh, no, it would not do at all!"

She wanted to laugh, but restrained the impulse. Whatever he and Beth had been up to, it certainly could not have involved a breach of good *ton*. She had never met a gentleman more concerned with propriety than Mr. Perkins. She allowed him to lead her to her seat, but extracted a reluctant promise for another dance later in the evening.

The poor man departed with such alacrity that Nell was filled with silent laughter. The happy gleam was still in her eye when she turned to find herself face to face with Sir Charles. The metallic glint in his own eye drained the cheerful brilliance from hers.

"Nell, I should like to apolo—" he began, only to be cut off as Lord Warwynne drew up with Beth on his arm to claim his waltz with Nell.

Without casting so much as a glance at Sir Charles, she went directly off with the fair viscount. For the rest of the evening no gayer lady could be found in Lady Harlowe's salons than Miss Eleanor Trant. She smiled, laughed, and teased gentlemen throughout dance after dance. If the gossips whispered about Miss Elizabeth Trant's chaperone, Nell did not listen. She whirled and twirled, chattered and charmed as if she were a young belle making her come-out. When not dancing, she was surrounded by a circle of admiring beaux, of whom Sir Charles Grayson was not a member.

Later, as she went into supper on Lord Warwynne's arm and sat down opposite her sister and the baronet, her bright smile wavered for just a moment. But a fresh glass of champagne restored it in full measure.

Afterward, she did not recall one item of the midnight supper, nor one word she exchanged with anyone. She only remembered—and this only too well!—the touch of Sir Charles's hand upon her calf, the press of his lips upon her ankle, and the rasp of his voice as he whispered her name.

But she thrust these memories aside and hid her hurt beneath a mask of gaiety that focused on everyone present except the gentleman so plaguing her thoughts. She forced herself to be cheerful, and somehow the hours passed and the ball ended and no one suspected how desperately unhappy she was.

# - 5 -

THE CARRIAGE DOOR clapped shut like the iron bars at Newgate. It took all of Nell's considerable will not to show by even the merest gesture that the journey homeward seemed an endless agony for her. The silence that fell between Sir Charles, Beth, and herself closed in upon her, suffocating her. She tried to pretend he was not there, but of course his body on the squabs of the seat opposite her dominated the small, darkened interior. No amount of pretense could disregard the nearness of his knee or the long, muscular leg resting just a whisper away from her own.

She did not know how she managed to survive the rest of the evening. It had all become a miserable masquerade for her, a nightmare of light, sound, and color. Her head ached from the effort of dissembling. She wished Beth would fill the silence with her cheerful prattle, but she too sat staring wordlessly into her lap.

The instant the carriage drew up before their town house in Mount Street, Nell bid Sir Charles a hasty goodnight and slipped from her seat to dart lightly up the steps. She heard Beth and Sir Charles exchanging words behind her, but did not pause to listen. She set her sights on the narrow stairway, seeking only the quiet refuge of her room. But as she gripped the balustrade, she was halted in mid-step by her mother's weary voice.

"Oh, there you are at last! I had quite given up hope of seeing you before dawn," Mrs. Trant drawled sleepily from the head of the stairs.

Nell's hand tightened on the mahogany railing. The door behind her opened, and, with the soft rustle of muslin, her sister came to stand next to her.

"Do come up and tell me about Lady Harlowe's ball," commanded their mother as she floated toward her bed-chambers. Her lace peignoir disappeared from view, and, sighing, Nell mounted the steps. The last thing she desired at this moment was a trying interview with Mama. She had meant to open Beth's eyes tonight, but instead her own had suddenly seen the true state of affairs. Even after three long years Sir Charles Grayson had not lessened his ability to wound her. More than anything she had wanted to fall into his arms, and now she sought desperately to forget him.

She was absorbed in her own thoughts as they entered their mother's ivory-and-gilt boudoir. Mrs. Trant reposed upon a backless chaise longue, the lavender lace of her peignoir spilling to the floor. Her arms were thrown out at the sides and her lids had dropped heavily over her eyes, as if the exertion of greeting her daughters had completely undone her. But as they took their places upon a pair of shabbily elegant straight-backed chairs, the lids came up and a glinting green gaze was directed at them.

"As it's nearing three, I do not doubt you enjoyed your-selves," she remarked on a sigh that was somehow a question.

"Yes, Mama," they chorused together. Beth went on to say the ball had been a monstrous crush, a mark of Lady Harlowe's success.

"Ah," said their Mama, languidly brushing her dark brown hair back with a squat hand. Nell's eyes followed the motion, then dropped rapidly to the worn carpet as her glance happened upon her mother's disconcertingly shrewd stare.

A short silence descended until Beth nervously inquired how Mama had enjoyed the Duchess of Cumberleigh's card-party.

"Her Grace exhibited an extreme want of manners, my

dear, by winning every hand," Mrs. Trant replied with rather more vigor than was her wont.

"Oh, Mama, did you go aground?" Nell immediately burst out.

Her mother once again relaxed against the frayed cushions of her chaise. "I hope, Eleanor, you are not instructing your charges in the use of such vulgarities," she chided placidly. "I was forced to pledge my bracelet—"

"Oh, Mama!" Nell interposed in a voice full of reproach.

"—but of course, once our Little Elizabeth is wed, I shall recover it from the Duchess." Eugenia Trant spoke without the least appearance of contrition.

"How can you?" demanded her eldest daughter instantly. Nell jumped up and paced back and forth in the room. "How can you even consider letting Sir Charles redeem your gambling losses? Is Beth to be sold for a *bracelet?*"

"Please sit down, Eleanor," her mother ordered, her voice unusually sharp. "The sight of your disordered flitting is altogether wearying. You have neither the right nor the least cause to judge your sister so harshly."

Nell shot a quick look at Beth, who had shrunk into the meager protection of her chair, her cornflower-blue eyes dark in a colorless face. Casting herself back against her own chair, Nell opened her mouth to renew her protest, but was outmaneuvered by Mrs. Trant, who closed her eyes and bid Elizabeth to tell her, if she pleased, about the ball.

As Beth rattled on, describing the decorations and the fashions, the dances and the supper, Nell was left to seethe in silence. Her head now felt rather as if a hunting party were galloping through it, and she longed for her bed, where she intended to put out of her mind all thought of Beth's betrothal, Mama's losses and, most of all, Sir Charles's perfidious charm. She was about to address her mother, then retire, when Mrs. Trant's eyes flew open and fixed themselves on her elder daughter.

"I trust you did not sit by the wall all night, Eleanor," she sighed with a lazy flutter of a lavender-wrapped arm.

"Sir Charles did not let her do so, Mama, I assure you," Beth answered readily. She had by this time regained both her color and her composure and thus went on easily. "Nell did insist on staying with the dowagers at first and poor Lord Warwynne was quite put out with her because she refused him so often, but you know Sir Charles. *He* was not dissuaded by Nell's refusals. He simply led her into a dance and afterward I vow Nell had more beaux than I. She was quite the belle, Mama."

"Yes," Mrs. Trant agreed on a drowsy nod. "Sir Charles is not the man to be easily set aside. In fact, he is the only man who could bring your sister to bridle. But in the end even he was thrown." She stifled another yawn as if the whole subject were putting her to sleep, calmly ignoring Nell's baleful glare.

"Really, Mama!" Nell expostulated on a hot breath. "If you mean to occupy yourself with such nonsensical prattle, I pray you will excuse me!"

She stormed to the door, pausing as Beth cried out, "Oh, Nell, we did not mean—" but her quick apology was silenced by a tap of her mother's hand.

"Let her go, let her go. Now, tell me again, what was it the Dowager Countess said to Mrs. Macclesfield?"

Eleanor slammed out of the boudoir in a huff. Once shut into her own room, she assaulted the creaky floorboard next to her bed with impatient strides. With each furious step, her anger mounted. She raged at her parents, who were so willing to bestow their younger daughter into the care of a man who did not love her; at Sir Charles for having the power to disrupt her every rational thought or action; and mostly at herself for her own folly in responding to his overwhelming masculinity. She despised her weakness and even the thought that it was merely a physical reaction, far removed from her heart, did not comfort her.

After a quarter hour, she could no longer contain her repressed rage. Grabbing a glass powder pot from the top of a wooden corner commode, Nell hurled it vigorously to the floor. The splintering crash seemed to uncoil the springs of her wound-up fury. She stared at the dust-spattered shards, her nostrils filling with the powdery scent of lavender, then drew a long, shuddering sigh and began calmly to collect the bits of glass from the besprinkled floor. One day, she knew, her dreadful temper would be the ruin of her.

The soft click of a door caught her attention as she was laying the last of the shattered glass onto the top of her vanity, and in a flash, Nell hurried into Elizabeth's small chamber. Beth's hands were raised to her curls, and her full lips parted in surprise at her sister's abrupt entrance. "I—I thought you'd gone to sleep," she stammered finally as her hands fell to her sides.

"Beth, are you falling in love with Sir Charles?" Nell asked without preamble. She had at last decided that if, indeed, Beth had formed a *tendre* for Grayson, then she was posting back to Norfolk without delay.

"W-what? S-sir Charles?" Beth sputtered feebly.

"Are you in love with him?" her sister demanded, striding forward.

Beth backed away slightly, then laughed nervously. "Wherever did you get such a notion, Nell? Of course I am not! I've told you, ours is to be a match of convenience—nothing more."

"But you looked like a woman in love tonight," Nell insisted, her voice clearly stating her disapproval. "And don't try to bamboozle me with some Banbury tale. You know you could never lie to me."

"But I'm not in love with Sir Charles!" Beth exclaimed, her body trembling.

The truth was writ plain upon her face, and for a moment Nell gazed at her, nonplused. Her young sister had never been able to hide her feelings. She'd clearly been moon-struck this evening, and if she did not love Sir Charles, what possible explanation could there be? As Nell studied Elizabeth with narrowed, speculative eyes, vermilion flags waved over her sister's cheeks. Nell recognized the apprehension she had noted once before, and her own eyes widened.

"Are you in love with someone else?" she inquired in disbelief.

A streak of blue flew across the room, Beth's arms were flung about Nell's neck, and the young woman sobbed into her shoulder. "D-don't tell, Nell, please!" she pleaded through her weeping. "I—it's not possible to love him. He has n-nothing to offer!"

Frantically searching her memory for an answer to this puzzle, Nell suddenly recalled her sister bent earnestly toward Mr. Perkins and with an astonished exclamation detached Beth from her shoulder to hold her out at arm's length.

"Are you saying—can you possibly mean?—Beth, are you in love with Josiah Perkins?" she demanded.

A fresh wail rose from Beth, and patiently Nell drew her to sit on the edge of a high, narrow bed and folded her within the comfort of her arms. Murmuring softly in a soothing voice, Nell tried to comprehend the fact that her silly sister would prefer Mr. Josiah Perkins to Sir Charles Grayson. Clearly, Elizabeth was cloth-headed.

At length, Beth's sobs eased, and Nell gently wiped the traces of tears from the girl's rounded cheeks. "Now, dear goose, please tell me about you and Mr. Perkins."

Stumbling at first, then gathering assurance as she spoke, Beth told Nell of her deep admiration for Mr. Perkins. "He is so estimable, so good, so noble! His is truly a worthy disposition," she summed up in rapturous tones.

Nell could only address her sister as if she were discoursing with a Bedlamite. Cautiously, she stemmed Beth's words of adulation. "But why is he ineligible?"

"He has no money, nor even many prospects at present," Beth explained mournfully. "He is Lord Harlowe's secretary."

"So that is how you knew he would be there tonight," Nell interrupted.

"Yes. He does not, as a rule, attend many such functions. He is far too serious-minded for frivolities, you know. But he was with Lord Harlowe at the Somerfields' last fall when Mama and I went to stay there."

"You came to know him there?" Nell probed.

"Oh, yes," Beth breathed in a glowing voice. "From the moment of introduction, I saw that Mr. Perkins was quite unlike other men. *He* does not care for wasting his time with gaming or sporting or—or with meaningless dalliance. We—we came to know each other . . . though, of course, not one impropriety passed between us."

*That* Nell could well believe, having made even so brief an acquaintance with the gentleman in question. "Have you seen him often since then?"

"No, no! We've had no assignations." The sigh that accompanied this most estimable declaration sounded almost wistful. "That's what made tonight so very special, you see."

"And do you think Mr. Perkins returns your regard?"

Nell inquired gently, intently watching her sister.

"I—I cannot be certain, though I have sometimes detected a certain warmth . . ." Beth replied with a shy blush. "Mr. Perkins is of far too superior a mind to speak where he knows he cannot."

"But whyever not?" Nell demanded briskly. "As Lord Harlowe's secretary, he must have means enough to provide for a wife."

"B-but nothing to equal the Graysons!" Beth stifled a small sob and continued in an uneven voice. "He is the son of a country clergyman, and there remain three other sons and two daughters to be settled. Even should Mr. Perkins desire to take a wife, it would be *years* before he could afford to do so. And he could *never* support his wife's family in addition to his own."

Nell inspected her sister's dismal countenance for some time, then stood and began pacing restlessly. At last she stopped in front of Beth. "You cannot be such a gudgeon as to marry Grayson when your affections are engaged elsewhere. We Trants shall manage to rub along without having to sacrifice you, Beth."

"You have been away for so long, Nell, that you do not realize what state we were in," Beth said tremulously. "It is all up with Papa. He was being dunned at every corner until Sir Charles stopped the creditors from hounding him. For months we did not dare go abroad for fear he would be presented with another vowel. We did without, Nell, in ways that would shock you. You have seen that all the servants are gone save Fowles and Mrs. Barrows. You must see that I could not be so ungrateful a daughter as to allow my personal inclinations to send Papa back into dun territory."

Beth rose with solemn dignity from the bedside and came to take Nell's hands in her own. "Do not be distressed on my account, I beg of you! I know my marriage is nothing but a Smithfield bargain. But I'm certain Sir Charles and I shall manage tolerably well together. He is all kindness to me, and that is more than many in my position could expect. Do not worry, Nellie, please! I accept my fate, I am satisfied, *truly* I am!"

Nell did not believe a word of it. The nobility of Beth's sacrifice was lost on her. Cold fury struck at her over her parents' selfish willingness to ruin Beth's chances for happiness. She needed to be alone before the rein on her temper was loosened further still.

Silently accepting her sister's kiss, Nell retreated swiftly to her room. She threw off her clothes without looking where she hurled them, then slipped between the muslin sheets to stare at the shadows pirouetting about her room.

Her anger slowly seeped away into the night as she lay considering all that she'd learned. All thought of posting back to her school vanished. She would stay in London until she discovered how she might best save Beth from forfeiting herself without pitching her father into ruin. If, indeed, he truly faced such a state, which Nell doubted.

Her other problem set her to trembling beneath the eiderdown coverlet. Sir Charles might be a rogue capable of breaking hearts as carelessly as the wind tosses leaves, but knowing his character did not prevent Nell from reacting to his physical magnetism. To remain in Town, she must renew her determination to avoid him at all costs. This, she told herself, should be the easiest of all things because she had not the least desire ever to see him again.

The last image that rose before her sleep-laden eyes was of a dark, curly head bent over the curve of her ankle, his lips pressing warmly against her silk stocking.

Nell tossed and turned all night and awoke heavy-eyed and melancholy the next morning.

But her resolutions had not dimmed. They had, in fact, grown even stronger. In keeping with her determination not to again set eyes upon Sir Charles Grayson, Nell closeted herself with Mrs. Barrows in the kitchens, selecting and discarding choices for the supper to be given for an intimate group, some thirty or so guests, on the night of her sister's ball. Then she found she must call upon several old friends and remained from home until close upon the hour to dine. Arriving to learn that Sir Charles was expected for supper, Nell retired directly to her room for the evening, claiming unaccustomed fatigue.

Her stratagem proved successful. By keeping a sharp eye on the street, Nell managed to disappear each time the baronet's carriage drew up. For the next two days, she avoided him quite easily, a fact which should have bolstered her spirits, but perversely had quite the opposite effect.

Nell was thus unaccountably blue-deviled when she left the Wedgwood warehouse in York Street on the third afternoon following the disastrous ball at Lady Harlowe's. She had not yet struck upon a method of untangling her sister's snarled heartstrings, and it was to this singular failure that Nell attributed her own downcast humor as she stepped unseeing down the noisy street.

She was startled from her melancholy reverie by the sound of her name and she halted, looking about her in a daze.

"Miss Trant," said the voice again, this time directly behind her.

She turned to find Mr. Josiah Perkins making her a rather stiff bow. "Good day, Mr. Perkins," she said, holding out her hand.

He took it briefly, eyeing the length of her outmoded pelisse of durable drabcloth, taking in the high-crowned cloth bonnet trimmed with yellow cording, and the worn muff that clearly had seen better days. In turn, Nell noted that Mr. Perkins carried himself with a calm assurance that had been lacking at their last meeting. The plain nut-brown jacket and fawn trousers became him far better than his evening wear had, and Nell concluded that the gentleman had not been in his element at the ball.

His hazel eyes cast about in a searching manner, and she followed them, puzzled as her gaze returned to him.

"Is your maid executing some errand, Miss Trant?" he asked solemnly.

A smile flitted across her mouth, but she managed to respond with creditable sobriety. "I am without a maid, sir."

"Then, of course, Miss Trant, you must permit me to give you my escort home."

Overcoming her impulse to laugh at the heavy frown gracing his features, she said levelly, "There is no need, sir, for you to inconvenience yourself on my behalf."

"It is no inconvenience," he insisted firmly. "I cannot allow a young lady of my acquaintance to wander the streets unescorted."

"I am quite beyond that age, sir, I assure you," Nell said with a light laugh. Really, he was quite absurd!

"Nonsense!" Mr. Perkins returned in an implacable voice. He presented her with his arm, and Nell saw no option but to take it.

As they walked, Nell inspected him with several quick sidelong glances and found much to admire in his regular features. His manner might be straitlaced and dull, but he raidated dependability. *He* would not keep a lightskirt, she decided with a surge of partiality. She focused a warm smile on him.

"I could not but notice your appraisal of my dress," Nell said quite easily, "and must beg you to excuse my dowdy state."

"Nothing of the sort!" he disagreed quickly. He looked at her with a gaze that inquired how she could have thought him capable of such a breach of etiquette. "If anything," he continued seriously, "I admire your ability to look so well-turned-out in a fashion quite obviously out of date."

Her lips curved upward at the backhanded compliment. "Thank you. But as I am somewhat rather more out of date than my pelisse, I trust you will realize I can see my own way home."

Her smile was met with Mr. Perkins's horrified disclaimer that she was certainly not "out of date." It occurred to Nell that, as provoking as he was, at least Sir Charles had the saving grace of a sense of humor. With a sigh, Nell tried a new tack.

"I do try to make my belongings last, Mr. Perkins. Raised as we were, Beth and I have learned how to economize. She would make an excellent wife for a man of limited means."

She felt him tense beside her, a sudden rigidity finding its way into his step, and was not surprised to discover a dull flush creeping over his face. He stared at the crowds ahead of them and made no response.

After a slight pause, Nell prodded, "But then, of course, fortune may provide Beth with no need to practice economy."

She peeped at him around the brim of her bonnet and noted that his flush had heightened. More than a devout declaration, Mr. Perkins's refusal to discuss Beth told Nell how deep his regard for her sister was. Satisfaction added a cheeriness to her voice as she airily began to converse upon the chill spring weather, to which Mr. Perkins returned only the most wooden responses.

# - 6 -

SLIPPING HER SHOES from her feet, Nell tucked herself into the corner of the sofa nearest the flickering fire and read the letter in her head. With a minimum of words, Miss Poole conveyed her understanding, tinged with regret, that her dear Eleanor would be remaining in London. She further intimated that she herself would post to Town should Miss Trant not return by the end of the school term. Though she could not say why, this prospect brought a slight frown to Nell's brow, and the letter dropped into the folds of her faded ensign-blue half-dress. Like most of her gowns, it was several years out of fashion, though the kerseymere frock still became her thin figure very well.

Her hand rubbed restively over her brow, as if she had in truth the headache she had claimed when she begged off accompanying the rest of her family to dine at Mrs. Macclesfield's. More than ever, Nell had felt the need of solitude. The satisfying knowledge that Mr. Perkins returned Beth's affection in full force had presented her with further problems to untangle. For as much as she meant to bring the pair of lovers together, Nell had not the least idea how to do so.

The question currently worrying her was how much of Beth's tale regarding Papa's finances was truth and how much exaggeration. She had no doubt that her malleable sister had been led deliberately to believe the family's straits far worse than they actually were. She knew precisely how much both her parents welcomed the alliance with the Graysons, and she also knew they would play upon Beth's sweetness and gullibility to get what they wanted. It was a coil that would take longer than she wished to unwind, and though she desired nothing more than to set aside these problems and return to Norfolk, for some inexplicable reason, Nell desired nothing less than to have her friend come to London.

Again she picked up the letter from Miss Poole. The hand was as thin and sparse as the author herself, the message as pragmatic. A picture of the very neat, very precise Drusilla rose from the vellum. She was but a year or so older than Nell, but Drusilla had never indulged in the follies of youth. Any chance remembrance of her younger years had been long suppressed. Perhaps this was why her colorless blond hair was already graying and deep lines marked the edges of her wide mouth. Thinking of her sensible, yet pertinacious friend, a warm smile touched Nell's lips.

The smile lingered as a light tap upon the door lifted her eyes from the page in her hand. It vanished upon perceiving the gentleman crossing the threshold.

That the disappearance of her smile annoyed Sir Charles was evident in the quick flash of anger that turned his eyes nearly as dark a black as his glossy hair.

"Ah—delighted to see me as always, Miss Trant?" he drawled.

The mockery that sat so strangely upon his strong face felt like a slap to Nell, and she tensed against the pang that shuddered through her. Extremely conscious of her unwanted response to his mere presence, she turned her head into the shadows and said tonelessly, "The family are gone to dine at Mrs. Macclesfield's."

"I know," he said shortly.

Her head whipped round at that, sending her loose red curls swaying, but his face, like his voice, was without expression. Why had he come?

"Then you must know you should not be here, Sir Charles. I am unchaperoned."

As if he did not hear her, the baronet drew farther into

the dimly lit room. Nell tried not to react to his graceful movement, but even as she told herself he was but a man like any other, her pulses leapt. To cover her confusion, she straightened and busied herself with tying on her jean half-boots.

"I have been trying to see you for days," Sir Charles remarked as he came to stand before her. "I wish to make my apologies for my behavior at Lady Harlowe's."

"There is no need," Nell said quickly, darting a glance up at him. Then, unable to resist, she added in honeyed tones, "You could not help yourself, I know."

His brow shot up, and he looked at her quizzically. She straightened slowly and explained primly, "Such flirtation has become so habitual with you, even you cannot control it."

"One of these days, my dear Eleanor," he said ominously, "I am going to have to play Petruchio to your Kate and teach you not to be such a shrew." Her outraged intake of breath drew a low laugh from him as he stretched himself easily onto a chair opposite her. "In truth, Nell, I did not mean to kiss you in such a manner that night. But I excuse myself with the thought that if you did not have such a lovely ankle, I would not have kissed it."

"Do you call this an apology?" she snapped, rising. The letter, which had again dropped onto her lap, slid soundlessly to the floor. Sir Charles eyed it casually, then more sharply as Nell bent swiftly—almost guiltily—to retrieve it.

"Love letters, my dear?" he taunted.

Refolding the missive, Nell threw him a scornful look. "It is from Miss Poole. Not that it's the least concern of yours."

"Ah," he drawled in a hateful voice. "Of course. I should have known. *You*, of course, would not receive love letters whilst Miss Poole is available to stand dragon."

"What do you mean by that?" she queried instantly. "And if you mean to begin another round of arguments, you will have to excuse me. I am not in the mood to listen to your ill-considered views."

Nell strode for the door, but a forceful grip on her wrist detained her. Furious, she swung to face her captor. "Let me go!" she hissed.

"Come, Nell, I did not mean to argue further with you," Charles said gently. "I'll release you if you will stay to talk with me."

Even as her resolve to quit the room faded, Nell resisted. "I cannot see that we have anything to discuss," she said crushingly.

The clasp about the cuff of her long sleeve tightened, then withdrew abruptly. As she watched Sir Charles cross to the grate, Nell wondered wildly if he had detected the frenzied coursing of her pulse, if he had realized the violent effect he wrought upon her senses. His back to her, Grayson hoisted the iron poker and aggressively attacked the remains of the logs in the grate. His actions had a stiffness that was at variance with his usual athletic grace, and she stared at the back of his burgundy coat with wonder.

He cast a quick, hard glance at her over his broad shoulder, then turning his attention once more to stoking the fire, he stated roughly, "I give you my word that there will be no repetition of my actions that night. I . . . regret them more fully than I can convey."

Nell's mouth fell open. Sincerity was plain in his voice. But something else was hidden there, something she could not quite define. As she stood staring in bemusement, he deposited the poker in its stand with a clang and turned to face her. Even in the indistinct light cast by the few tapers of a single candlelabrum, she could see that the cynical gleam had disappeared from his gaze. A slight lift of his heavy brow brought her lips together.

"Very well, Sir Charles. Your apology is accepted," Nell said, as one conferring a great honor. "And now I pray you will excuse me . . ."

"But I won't," he countered. "Stay a moment, Nell— Miss Trant, if you please."

He favored her with his most irresistible smile, but his eyes remained darkly serious and his taut stance bespoke his determination to detain her. Whatever his reasons, it was clear Sir Charles meant to speak with her. With a disgruntled sigh, Nell resumed her seat upon the sofa. He again took up his place across from her. For a time they eyed one another warily in a strained silence.

Then on a sudden impulse Nell leaned forward, her trans-lucent beauty outlined against the firelight as she burst out,

"Why on earth are you claiming Beth for your wife?"

"Can you not come to accept me for your brother-in-law?" he asked in a guarded reply.

"No."

"Why do you disapprove so?"

"Because you do not love her," Nell answered promptly. "And more, because she does not love you. One love might perhaps beget another, but where there is none between you, I fear your chance of success in this marriage to be slim indeed."

Sir Charles made a careful study of his well-trimmed nails. Very slowly he said, "I have already settled a vast deal of money upon your father, my dear."

The color fled from her face. So Beth had not exaggerated after all. Nell bent her head. "Oh."

"He was at point nonplus, Nell," Charles explained quietly. Without looking up she was aware of his piercing scrutiny. She refused to meet his gaze, and after a time, he went on. "It is time I married. My mother fears she'll not live to see the Grayson line continue. I do not seek a love match and want no wife to expect it. Your sister fully understands the reasons for our bargain."

Nell nodded dumbly. A visible shiver convulsed through her slim frame. Whatever could she do? The thought of Sir Charles covering Papa's debts made her feel sick. "Poor Beth," she thought dully, not realizing her thought had become a whisper. She raised her head in time to catch a flicker of pique traverse his face, but it fled so quickly before the inscrutable mask that settled there that Nell doubted she had seen it at all.

"There could be an . . . alternative," Sir Charles said without expression.

A sudden suspicion colored her eyes an opaque green, but she refrained from comment.

"If you so dislike the idea of my marrying Miss Elizabeth," he continued, watching her intently, "we could resolve the matter easily enough."

"How?" she asked, her body stiffening with distrust. If he dared to offer Beth a Carte Blanche . . .

He startled this unjust thought from her by suggesting in a carefully toneless voice. "Marry me instead, Nell."

"What!" she stared at him in stunned disbelief. Not in

her wildest imaginings had she expected such an offer! She barely heard him as he bent forward to speak.

"I am in need of a wife. Your family has need of my wealth. We could have an arrangement—"

"An arrangement!" she broke in, fairly leaping to her feet. "Is that all you understand? Do you honestly believe that I would sell myself to you for the sake of—of your *money?*" she sputtered, her eyes sparking dangerously.

He came lithely to stand before her. "No," he replied harshly. "But for the sake of your sister, I think you might."

"It is impossible!" Nell declared hotly. She was trembling from head to foot with a sickening rage. That he would offer for her in place of Beth as casually as one might change horses in a harness made her ill. She felt the heat of her anger stain her cheeks and struggled for control. "I cannot believe you would suggest it! Love should bring two people together, Sir Charles—but of course, that is a notion far beyond your comprehension."

"Oh, I fully understand the state of love," he bit back. "That hellish torture that you women employ to torment mankind! I removed myself from the list of eligible victims some time ago, my dear, and do not intend to offer myself up again. It is the honor of my name and my wealth I am offering—"

"Honor!" she cut in, then had the pleasure of seeing him flush darkly. "It is clear to me, Sir Charles, that three years' time has done nothing to dim your arrogant conceit!"

"And it is clear to me," he returned through tight lips, "that it has done little to cure you of intemperance!"

"Oh! *You* dare to accuse *me* of intemperance!" she cried.

"Yes, I do! You are self-indulgent to excess, caring for no one but yourself!"

For a frozen instant they glared at one another, then Nell summoned up her poise and swept to the door. As she took hold of the handle, an imperative "Miss Trant!" halted her.

She pivoted stiffly. "Yes?"

"You would not wish to chance losing your letter from your dear Miss Poole," he said with heavy sarcasm.

She stared with rigid hostility at his still-flushed face, then stretched out her hand to snatch the letter from his. About to exit, she paused. "Whyever must you mock her so?" she asked with a touch of sadness in her voice. "Drusilla

Poole has stood my friend for many years. I can think of
no reason for you to hold her in dislike."

"No reason why..." Sir Charles echoed blankly. He
looked at her for a long moment as if she had suddenly
acquired a second head, then recovered the practiced mask
of cynicism and said with a hint of boredom, "You wrong
me, my dear. I do not hold Miss Poole in dislike. I do not,
in fact, hold Miss Poole in anything at all."

"Oh!" Nell exclaimed with a stamp of her foot. "You
are insufferable!"

She wrenched open the door and retreated to her room.
It took her no little while to calm her raging pulses. Not
only had the baronet crassly insulted her friend, her family
and herself, but he had also played upon her every weakness!
Igniting the hot temper he knew she possessed, inflaming
the desires he knew she could not deny! He was a scoundrel
of the basest sort, and it disgusted Nell to consider that she
had—for the barest moment, to be sure, but still she had—
wanted very much to accept the terms of his "arrangement."
She could not understand herself, and, it was obvious, she
could no longer trust herself.

By the time the rest of her family returned from Mrs.
Macclesfield's, Nell had the headache in earnest. She placed
the blame solely upon Sir Charles's shoulders, for she had
gone round and round their confrontation until her head
whirled. Her greatest puzzlement came from his disclosure
that he had removed himself as a "victim of love." Had he
meant he had done so before their betrothment ended or
because of it? Sometimes she told herself fiercely she did
not care a rap which it was, but at others she thought she
would go mad if she did not discover the truth behind it.

As she was trying unsuccessfully once more to shove
these disturbing questions from her mind Elizabeth slipped
quietly into her darkened bedchamber.

"Nell, dearest, are you feeling unwell?" Beth whispered
tentatively.

Longing to be alone, yet having no desire to be further
beleaguered by her thoughts, she answered after a bare
pause, "No. I still have the headache, that is all."

"Still? Oh, you poor thing!" her sister said in quick
sympathy. She flew to Nell's side. "Shall I prepare a tisane
for you? Or perhaps fetch some of Mama's laudanum?"

"No, no, I have no wish to be physicked," Nell protested.

Beth hesitated, then at last perched herself on the edge of the bed. "As you wish, dear one," she said as she toyed with the pleated ruffles of her primrose gown. "You did not tell me, Nell," she added with forced casualness after a slight pause, "that you met with Mr. Perkins this afternoon."

Nell smiled into the night shadows. "No, I didn't, and wonder therefore how you came to know of it."

"Lord Harlowe took ill this evening and his secretary attended Lady Harlowe in his stead," Beth explained, striving vainly for a neutral tone. "He was very much disturbed to discover you wandering in York Street unescorted, and truly, Nell, you know you should not have done so."

"Perhaps not," Nell agreed, credibly managing to keep the amusement out of her voice. Mr. Perkins was, without doubt, she decided, the prosiest creature alive. "And beyond dissecting the follies of my behavior, did the pair of you discuss much else?"

"We spoke a little of the shocking tale of Lord Byron and Claire Clairmont—but only in passing," she added hastily, "for Mr. Perkins does not indulge in idle gossip. And you must not think that he paid me any *particular* attention, for he has too much sensitivity to expose me to any talk."

Beth's speech was colored with her admiration. It was obvious that the estimable Mr. Perkins did not strike her in the least as dull. It occurred to Nell that only a woman deeply in love could overlook such a major flaw in his character.

Shifting her weight, she propped herself up on her elbow and stared through the darkness at her sister. Choosing each word carefully, she said in a voice not quite steady, "You cannot marry Sir Charles, Beth. It is unfair to both of you to do so when your heart is bestowed elsewhere."

Beth's head turned away, completely hidden behind the soft veil of her brown hair. "Please don't hector me further on this subject," she begged. "It cannot change my mind, and it serves only to inflict a pain I am sure you would not wish upon me."

Though she flinched at the gentle rebuke, Nell did not mean to give way. "He came tonight while you were away."

"Sir Charles? Here? Tonight?"

"Yes, and he put forth a suggestion," Nell said, her voice

hardening at the memory. "He thought perhaps it might suit if I were to become his wife in your stead."

"Oh!" Beth said weakly. For a long instant, she held her breath, then inquired as she expelled it on a long sigh, "And what did you say?"

"Say?" Nell repeated in some heat. "I told him it was impossible, of course!"

"Oh," said Beth again, this time with flat disappointment.

"Dearest, dearest," Nell said, sitting upright with a little flurry, "you must see that it is impossible! Why, he insulted both of us by even suggesting such a thing! He does not offer his heart—if he has one, which I take leave to doubt—but only his name, his money."

"Both of which are considerable," Beth returned with more spirit than was her wont. "I have tried to explain, time and again, but you willfully refuse to believe that Papa has landed us all into the River Tick."

Nell fell back onto her bed. Staring at the ceiling, she said tonelessly, "So Sir Charles confirmed. But I will find a way clear for us without having to throw either of us into that man's clutches."

Even in the darkness, Beth's distress communicated itself clearly. Her lips trembled and her voice shook. "Why can you not see that it is Sir Charles's kindness that is saving our family? We owe him a debt of gratitude worth far more than Papa's vowels, yet you heap nothing but scorn upon him. What have you become, Nell? You did not used to be such a cruel judge."

Nell's astounded silence followed Beth's impassioned speech, so unlike Beth's timid nature that neither could find words. Then, with a smothered sob, Elizabeth leapt up and whisked from the room. Nell did not go after her, but continued to lie gazing unseeing at the ceiling.

The child her sister had been when Nell had removed to Norfolk had vanished. Beth was a woman now and it seemed, more of a woman than any of them had suspected. Sitting up, Nell drew her knees in to clasp them with her arms, and rested her chin on them, pondering whether she ought to cease interfering after all. Beth had made her choice and what right did Nell have to say it was right or wrong? Then she suddenly recalled Beth's glowing tones in speaking of Mr. Perkins, and Nell knew without further doubt that it would be wrong to stand by and let her sister throw herself away, even for the good of the family.

Beth and Mr. Perkins had not, after all, had many opportunities to be together, to realize fully the depth of their regard for one another. Perhaps if they were thrown together more, the force of their own desires would convince them that they were meant for one another.

Nell fell asleep while mentally composing a note inviting Mr. Josiah Perkins to take tea.

# - 7 -

"HUMPH! ER—THAT is to say," Horace Trant stammered gruffly as he sidled his rotund figure toward the door.

Nell cut short his escape by wagging a finger under his bulbous nose. "Do not think to put me off, Papa! I mean to have it out of you," she declared with resolution. "Just how much money have you received from Sir Charles?"

Mr. Trant twisted his head, seeking a means of retreat from this unpleasant discussion. The curve of his chin settled farther into the folds of his cravat, and he fixed a longing gaze on the brandy decanter atop the sideboard. Like an untamed spirit, his eye darted on, sliding past Eleanor's stormy visage to run hither and thither.

"Er—you wouldn't care for a bit of breakfast, m'dear?" he offered as a condemned man pleading for a stay of execution.

"Papa!" his daughter rasped in dangerously low tones.

Nell took a menacing step forward, and he backed away, sputtering, "Well, well, I was badly dipped, you know, m'dear, very badly dipped."

"How badly dipped, Father?" came the relentless demand.

He halted, his back pressed against the striped wall of the breakfast room. Running a hand nervously through his thick gray mane and looking at everything except his daughter, he supplied on a huff, "A matter of twenty thousand or so, my dear."

*Twenty thousand!* Nell blanched and froze, stripped of all power to move. Grabbing his opportunity, Mr. Trant eased his bulk past her and departed, muttering something about his club as he went. She did not stop him. She did nothing, in fact, for the next several minutes. She had never dreamed of such a sum! How could it have happened?

Sinking slowly into a chair, she propped her elbows on the oval table and covered her face in her hands, suppressing an hysterical gurgle of laughter. Twenty thousand! She had thought to offer her father what was left of her inheritance and now could only shake her head at her own foolishness. Her three thousand pounds would be mere pocket-change to a man like Sir Charles Grayson. Even if she sold the school—which, of course, she could never do—she could never cover such a sum.

A moan escaped her, and she gradually let her hands fall from her face. Knowing the full extent of their indebtedness to Sir Charles changed nothing, nothing! She would still free Beth and somehow retrieve Papa's vowels from the baronet, even if she herself had to make a market marriage to do it. Her sister might view Sir Charles as a noble, generous man, but Nell knew better, and she would see them all in debtor's gaol before she'd permit him to take control of her family! She marched out of the room, more than ever determined to untangle the web Sir Charles had bound around her family.

Thus it was that Miss Trant smiled graciously at Mr. Josiah Perkins and offered him a second cup of tea that afternoon. As she poured, she watched Beth through lowered lashes and was satisfied. The rosebuds blooming on her sister's cheeks, the sparkle shining in her pastel eyes, convinced Nell anew that her plan was sound.

Handing the porcelain cup back to Mr. Perkins, she said warmly, "It is commendable of you, sir, to be carrying the expense of your younger brothers' schooling. I admire your generosity."

The gentleman reddened and said quickly, "It is only what every man in my position would do, Miss Trant. There is no need for your admiration, I assure you."

"Oh, but far too many would shirk their duty, sir," she returned, leaning forward in her enthusiasm and continuing earnestly. "That you are not puffed up with your charity only makes you the more worthy."

Mr. Perkins shifted uncomfortably. Beth stared at the hands clenched together in her lap. Nell made a great show of looking at the bronze clock on the mantelpiece, then exclaimed, "Oh, my, it is past three o'clock, and I have yet to inspect the supper menu with Mrs. Barrows!" She stood as she spoke and moved rapidly toward the door. "I shan't be but a moment, if you both will excuse me."

"It was time I was taking my leave in any case," said Mr. Perkins. He had properly risen with Nell and now set his cup on the table beside his chair. "I must thank you—"

Mentally grinding her teeth, Nell smiled broadly and cut in briskly, "No, no, Mr. Perkins. Do stay and keep Elizabeth company whilst I am gone. I assure you I shall return more quickly than takes time to tell."

"But of course I must go," he persisted. "I could not possibly remain *alone* with Miss Elizabeth." He bowed stiffly before Beth as he bid her good day, then moved to do the same before Nell.

Admirably restraining her utmost desire to strike him, Eleanor gave him her hand and said calmly, "You are so good, sir, to take such care with my sister's name. But I shall let you go only upon receipt of your promise to call upon me tomorrow. We could perhaps go for an outing in the Park."

"Uh—well—of course," agreed the unfortunate Mr. Perkins.

"Good, I shall see you tomorrow then. Shall we say at four?"

It was apparent that Mr. Perkins thought her a shocking flirt. His distaste for her boldness was stamped clear upon his face, but he nodded and gratefully took back his hand. Nell opened the door for him, knowing she was further distressing his sensibilities, and waved him out, then turned to note a deep sorrow cross Beth's round face. As if she did not see it, Nell grinned brightly and said cheerfully, "Well, Mr. Perkins is certainly an estimable man. I quite see why you like him as you do, Beth."

"You do?" her sister queried in a ghostly tone.

"Oh, yes. He is quite the most worthy gentleman of my acquaintance," she said with simple truth. "It is a pity, is it not, that he may be doomed to bachelorhood? I am assured that no man could make a more excellent husband than Mr. Perkins."

"You are?" Beth responded in that same lifeless voice.

"Indubitably," Nell pronounced as she stepped from the room.

Making her way back to the kitchens, she sighed heavily. Her task was obviously going to be burdened by the lack of complicity on the part of the lovers-to-be. If only, she thought with a spurt of resentment, Mr. Perkins weren't so very conventional! He could do with a little of Sir Charles's rakish attitudes. *Then* her problems would be solved, for the baronet would not worry over such dull matters as a woman's reputation. Oh, no, *he* would grasp every opportunity presented to be alone with the woman he loved! With such a thought in mind, she decided on a dinner menu.

When Mr. Perkins duly arrived the next day, Nell was in better spirits. She had chosen her very best day dress for the outing, a jaconet muslin with a deep flounce and a high ruff of a pale sea-green that softened the color of her eyes and deepened the red of her hair. Over this she had had to drape her dull drabcloth pelisse, but as the April weather had not yet warmed sufficiently for her to do otherwise, Nell gave in to practicality. Bonneted and ready to set out, with her hand resting lightly on Mr. Perkins's arm, she turned to take leave of her mother, who was lounging on the frayed sofa in the morning room. Nell was interrupted by Elizabeth's sudden appearance.

"Oh, Beth, dear," Nell said airily, "you are just in time to say good day to Mr. Perkins. We are to stroll through the Park, you know."

"Yes. Good day, Mr. Perkins," she said coolly.

Beth did not so much as glance at her sister, and Nell smiled inwardly at her sister's obvious jealousy. If only the silly chit would realize what that jealousy meant! Taking pity on her at last, Eleanor paused in the threshold, turning slightly. "If you are not engaged for the afternoon, Beth, why not come with us? You would enjoy the fresh air, and I'm certain Mr. Perkins would not object. Would you, sir?"

"Not in the least," he agreed promptly.

Beth's face lit up with sudden eagerness. "Oh, I should like that above all things! That is, if you don't mind being left alone, Mama," she added with a glance of dismay at her mother.

"Not at all. I've just been thinking how much I should enjoy a little cat-nap." Mrs. Trant yawned obligingly.

Before the last word was out, Elizabeth was dashing past them with a promise not to keep them waiting overlong. Smiling tenderly at her sister's ardent acceptance of her plans, her hand still in possession of Mr. Perkins's arm, Nell glanced up to discover herself staring at Sir Charles Grayson.

Looking over his shoulder as if to discover from whence he had materialized, she glimpsed Fowles, who gave her an apologetic expression. She dismissed the elderly servant with a wordless nod, then reluctantly dragged her eyes back to the baronet's face.

His brows raised as he moved his eye with meaningful deliberation from Nell's hand to her face. Feeling inexplicably guilty, she removed her hand from Mr. Perkins's sleeve as if it had suddenly scorched her. Then she scowled at the triumphant satisfaction on Sir Charles's features and strove not to compare the elegant turn-out of his black claw-hammer coat and dove-gray pantaloons with Mr. Perkins's nondescript frock coat and trousers. She returned her regard to the less fortunate of the two gentlemen and bestowed upon him a smile of dazzling warmth.

"Sir Charles, do come in," Mrs. Trant bade drowsily. As he leisurely strolled forth to bend over her extended hand, she added, "Our dear Elizabeth was about to accompany Eleanor and Mr. Potkins—"

"Perkins," Nell interjected peevishly.

"Ah, yes," agreed her mother with a nod. "But now that you have come, she will, of course, wish to stay."

Entering the room in time to hear her mother's pronouncement, Beth's happy smile faded, and her blue eyes went black with disappointment. Her figure, becomingly covered in a lemon-yellow cloth pelisse caped in the latest fashion, sagged visibly. "G-good day, Sir Charles," she stammered breathlessly. "I—I did not expect to see you this afternoon."

Sensing the sudden stiffening in Mr. Perkins's stance and heartily wishing Sir Charles to the devil, Nell stretched her lips in a tight smile and again bid her mother good day. She extended her gloved hand to retake Mr. Perkins's arm, but it hung in midair at the sound of the baronet's smooth voice.

"But why do we not all go together?" he suggested. "Fortunately I've come in my phaeton, which has more than enough room for the four of us."

"Oh, yes," Beth instantly concurred, while Mr. Perkins nodded his silent endorsement. "That is a lovely notion, Sir Charles."

Nell thought it something less than lovely, but being a lady, she refrained from expressing her view. Instead, she contented herself with a heated glare thrust over her shoulder as she agreed calmly. "If, that is, you should care to ride, Mr. Perkins," she added with a warm look cast up at the gentleman, hoping vainly for support.

Mr. Perkins, however, asserted his readiness to ride, and the four then took their leave of Mrs. Trant. Throughout the short drive to Hyde Park, Nell more than made up for the silence of the other three with her effervescent chatter. She leaned close to Mr. Perkins, who slid as near to the edge of the carriage seat as possible, and she gaily informed them all of her views on Lord Liverpool's handling of the government, on the lastest episode in *l'affaire Byron*, on, in fact, whatever came into her head. By the time the phaeton turned onto the tree-lined row of the park promenade, her sister was looking at her with something akin to animosity, while Mr. Perkins resembled a man riding in a tumbril on his way to the guillotine. Only Sir Charles remained affable as he smiled at her with an open amusement that set Nell's teeth on edge.

Bidding his driver to stop the carriage, the baronet offered his opinion that the day had been made for taking a stroll, and he descended without awaiting any other view to be expressed. He held his hand out for Beth to step down, then repeated the action for a coldly receptive Nell. No sooner had her feet touched the ground than Sir Charles was tucking her hand under his arm and setting forth, leaving

Mr. Perkins to escort Beth. As this was the very thing she most wanted, Nell's protest died on her lips. She walked with her back staunchly erect, her gaze settled firmly on the path before her.

"Do you mean to give me the go-by for the whole of our lives, Miss Trant?" Sir Charles inquired with interest. "Or merely for the rest of the day?"

"You must not speak such foolishness, Sir Charles. I have not refused to recognize you," Nell said in a voice dripping with acid. "You must think me very ill-bred, indeed, to suggest such a thing."

The look she shot him from beneath the brim of her bonnet told him precisely *who* she thought ill-bred, but with a low chuckle Sir Charles denied any such notion. "Come, Miss Trant, I thought we had agreed not to deal one another further blows. I admit to my boorish behavior, and I beg that you will once again have the graciousness to forgive my ill temper on the last occasion that we met."

His manner suggested a levity that Nell considered wholly misplaced, but she failed to maintain her resentment. With a sigh of resignation she bowed her head in a grand gesture of forgiveness.

"Ah, that's better," the baronet said jovially. "Now I desired to walk with you, my dear, so that we might discuss a matter of some delicacy."

Her head whipped round, renewed hostility glinting in her emerald eyes.

"Don't fly up into the boughs, Nell! I meant only that I wish to ask your opinion on what I should select as a betrothment gift for Beth," he explained with a hint of laughter.

Embarrassment slowly tinted Nell's face a becoming pink. "Oh. Well, I am certain you know best what sort of gift to select. After all," she added waspishly, "you've had *years* of experience at that sort of thing."

At first he did not comment, and Nell chanced a glimpse up at him just as he happened to look down at her. Their eyes met and held for a breathless moment. But the fierce brilliance in his blue gaze disconcerted Eleanor, compelling her to turn away.

"You must take care, my dear," Sir Charles chided mildly. "You've acquired quite an adder's tongue over the last three years. It wouldn't do, you know, to set people's backs up with your caustic remarks."

His rebuke stunned Nell. Her sister had accused her of being harsh and cruel, and now *he* again reproached her as a shrew! Had she indeed become so embittered? She felt a hot flush spread up her neck and over her face and bent her head penitently.

"Miss Elizabeth is quite . . . young," the baronet continued gently, "and I would greatly value your opinion on the matter of a gift."

"I—Elizabeth has little jewelry. Nothing ornate, mind you, but something simple, elegant," Nell said with a rush. "Perhaps a strand of pearls or a single diamond pendant. You know the sort of piece."

"Yes, thank you."

They continued to stroll along wordlessly, the breeze occasionally presenting them with the sound of the conversation occurring behind them, neither looking at the other. For Nell it was a bittersweet reminder of walks they had shared in the past, and she searched her mind frantically for a way to erase such memories from her thoughts. Unexpectedly the baronet came to her rescue by making several unexceptional observations on the weather. Then Sir Charles calmly presented her with a question that made her stop in her tracks.

"What did you say?" she demanded.

"I asked you, my dear," he said as he took her elbow and propelled her further down the path, "just what this fellow Perkins means to you."

Stopping yet again, Nell could only stand and stare at him in disbelief. She had no answer to such a question. It was so unexpected, so absurd! Sir Charles's face was expressionless, almost immobile, and his lids shuttered his eyes from her inspection. Without the least idea as to the reason behind his question, Nell said defensively, "I'm sure it's no business of yours, sir, what I think of Mr. Perkins or anyone else."

"I'm sure it's not," Sir Charles agreed, again taking her arm and moving forward. "I thought perhaps you might confide in me."

"You!" she exclaimed in surprise.

A wry twist of his lips met this interruption. "As your

friend, Nell, as well as a future member of your family. Now, before you present me with your views on my ineligibility to both states, let me tell you that, whatever has happened between us in the past, whatever will happen in the future, I shall always stand your friend, whether you wish it or no."

An unwonted prickling stung her eyes, and Nell looked quickly away, staring into the distance at gorgeous equipages driven by bewigged coachmen and filled with celebrated beauties and dandies which were beginning to fill the paths of the Park as the Fashionable Hour approached. What could Sir Charles mean by this? she asked herself and received no answer. She tried to concentrate on the budding leaves of the trees, but all she could think of was the caressing tone in which Sir Charles had declared himself her friend.

She was not allowed to indulge further in her reflections. A gentleman mounted on a long-tailed gray horse hailed their party as he drew up. With a quick motion, Viscount Warwynne dismounted and bowed to both ladies.

"Your servant," he said, running belligerent brown eyes over the baronet before turning back to present Miss Trant with a smile full of unmistakable yearning. "The Fates are kind indeed to bequeath upon me this chance meeting."

"Thank you, my lord, for quite the prettiest compliment I've ever received," Nell responded with a laugh that sounded for all the world like a coquette's promise.

The lanky viscount beamed, then was distracted by the restive tugging of his horse. Grasping the reins tightly, he ventured solemly, "I do trust, Miss Trant, that we shall be seeing you at Drury Lane this week. In fact, I would be honored if you would occupy my box there this Friday next."

"How thoughtful, Lord Warwynne," Nell said, ignoring the frown Sir Charles was casting upon her. This was a prime opportunity, indeed, and she bestowed her prettiest smile upon the viscount as she went on. "I am certain we are all grateful to you. We shall be happy to accept your kind offer, shan't we?"

She turned to include them all in her acceptance while his lordship strove to conceal his displeasure at this unexpected amplification of his invitation. His horse stirred again, sending his arm jerking upward, and, with a gesture of impatient apology, he bid them all good afternoon and remounted. Happily watching him ride off, Nell began planning precisely how she would arrange the seating in the theater box to best accommodate her plans for Beth and Mr. Perkins. In her abstraction, she ignored the speculative eye the baronet ran over her and the disapproval in her sister's face.

Turning to stroll back toward their phaeton, nodding graciously to acquaintances, Nell turned over in her mind just which gown suited Beth to perfection, just how she would require Mr. Perkins to escort Beth during the intermission. Studying the pair now walking before her, she considered that they were much better suited all round— why, Beth would look positively ridiculous beside the tall baronet! This gratifying observation deepened the satisfied curve to her lips.

Nell awoke from her brown study to discover that her steps had slowed and that the pair walking ahead had somehow increased the distance between them. The hand at her elbow explained the cause for this, but not the reason and she halted altogether to fix a questioning look upon Sir Charles.

He seemed to hesitate; then, with an imperceptible shrug, remarked almost casually, "The young viscount is in a fair way to being besotted with you, Miss Trant."

His statement amused her. It had been such a long time since she had been the object of masculine adoration that Eleanor couldn't help but respond to it. "Yes, I know," she agreed with a hint of smug contentment in her voice.

Sir Charles's heavy brows snapped together. "He is but a halfling, Nell," he pointed out severely. "He's scarcely out of leading strings!"

"Lord Warwynne," Nell rejoined in biting tones, "is somewhat older than Elizabeth, yet no one objects to your alliance with *her*."

"That is altogether different."

"I'm afraid I disagree, sir. I find it is quite similar."

Before he could respond, Nell stepped quickly after the receding form of her sister, her head held high and her heart beating uncommonly fast. He had claimed to be her friend, yet he chose to upbraid her constantly on matters that were not the least bit his conern. It was as if he meant to torment her for having had the extreme lack of sense to have once imagined herself in love with him. He was beside her now, his long strides easily matching her quick pace, but Nell refused to notice him, refused to acknowledge the sensations flooding her. Instead she channelled all her energy into feeding the fires of her anger. At least her temper could be relied on to resist Sir Charles Grayson's devilish charm.

# - 8 -

PREPARING TO ATTEND the Theatre Royal in Drury Lane, Nell donned her cream India muslin with the copper threading and vowed not to recollect the last evening on which she had worn the gown. But when she gazed into her reflection, she did not see a tall, slim, fashionably attired woman. She saw once again a dark head bent over the hem of her skirt, she felt the fingers caressing the white silk of her stocking, and she knew again the wave of longing that had crested through her. With a furious shake of her head that tossed the ivory feathers in her hair, Nell turned away from the cheval mirror and swept up her shawl and fan.

She would not allow herself to think of him! During the last week her appetite had faded and she had slept only fitfully. When not haunted by incessant visions of Sir Charles, she had been hounded by the implacable specter of twenty thousand pounds. Unable to rid herself of these images, she had become more uneasy with each passing day.

She and Sir Charles had been unable to meet even briefly without exchanging barbed comments. All attempts by Nell to avoid contact with him had been thwarted by her Mama, who insisted the baronet be consulted on each of the preparations for the upcoming ball and wedding to follow. Each meeting served to sharpen the pointed insults that passed between them, while increasing Nell's vulnerability to Sir Charles's most cutting quips. But not for the world would she let anyone discover how deeply his barbs had pierced her. She covered her inner pain with the gayest, most abandoned pursuit of pleasure in which she had ever indulged.

She had gone driving with Lord Warwynne no less than four afternoons out of five and stood up with him for three dances, including a waltz, just last evening at Sally Jersey's. Her attempts to secure Mr. Perkins's attendance upon her, and therefore upon Beth, had been less successful. He had held steadfastly that he could not neglect his post as Lord Harlowe's secretary, and she had had to content herself with his promise to accompany them to the theater tonight.

True to his word, Mr. Perkins awaited them in the Trants's small, shabbily formal sitting room. As always, it struck Nell upon seeing him that she would not have recognized him in a crowd and, because the thought smote her conscience, she greeted him more effusively than she might otherwise have done.

"Dear Mr. Perkins! How good it is to see you at last! You must not remain such a stranger to us, you know, for I vow you are sorely missed."

He took the hand she held out to him and mumbled an awkward greeting as he bent over it. Staring into the cropped brown hair, an unwanted comparison rose in her mind's eye of carelessly brushed ebony curls, and, with a fixed, bright smile, Nell bade him warmly to be seated. In the meantime, Elizabeth had seated herself stiffly on the edge of an uncomfortable lyre-back chair, carefully spreading out the skirt of her white gauze gown so as not to crush the ornately puckered hem. Nell had chosen the frock for her because its blue stripes precisely matched the color of Beth's eyes when she was at her most animated, which unfortunately she was not at the present time. She said nothing, merely nodded a civil greeting to Mr. Perkins, who returned the gesture with an aloof air. After this inauspicious beginning to the evening, a sense of gloom pervaded the trio.

Gloom rapidly gave way to doom with the appearance of Fowles to announce Sir Charles Grayson. No sooner had the baronet crossed the threshold than Nell remarked to the room in general what a pity it was that the evening's company could not have been more select.

"I quite agree, Miss Trant," Sir Charles said instantly in an affable voice belied by the taut bow he presented her. "But as Lord Warwynne expressly wished for you to come, we could do little but acquiesce after all."

The pleasantly delivered shot went directly to its mark. Nell quivered with resentment and only barely found voice with which to respond. "It is said, sir, that a true gentleman knows his own worth. What a pity you are so unaware of yours."

"Ah, but there, ma'am, you misjudge me," he returned easily. "I know to a groat what I am worth, and it is considerably more than twenty thousand pounds."

The sudden pallor of Nell's skin was exceeded only by Beth's. The younger woman had gone white with the first insult slung and now gripped the thin arms of her chair in an effort to cease her trembling. Deep concern shadowing his hazel eyes, Mr. Perkins quickly intervened.

"Did you not say, Miss Trant, that your mother was to make a member of this evening's party?"

For an instant Nell did not answer him, for she sat as if she had not heard him, her hands curled tightly around her closed fan, and her eyes fastened on the toe of her satin slipper. At last she raised her head to gaze dully at him.

"Yes," she said on a carefully controlled note. "But as Mama has never had the least notion of time, I doubt we shall see anything of her for quite some while yet."

Her eyes shifted unwillingly to where the baronet stood before the firegrate, then immediately darted away from the blinding intensity of his gaze. It was the same hard, penetrating look he had focused on her upon her first arrival in London, and the ferocity of it robbed her of breath. She fiddled with the ends of her silk ribbons, telling herself it did not matter how handsomely his deep blue coat displayed his fine figure, nor to what advantage his legs showed in the tight black pantaloons. And if his snowy white cambric shirt deepened the tan on that square face, it was a matter of the veriest indifference to her.

Such miserable musings were thankfully interrupted by her mother's dramatic entrance. Eugenia Trant had bedecked herself in the finest green satin, which shimmered like dewy grass as she floated into the room. Her Austrian cap of satin and blonde sat tipped slightly askew, perhaps to balance the lopsided hanging of her laced shawl over her left arm. Everyone rose as she entered, but she urged them back into their seats with a desultory wave.

"I must *rest* for a moment, if you please," she explained with a long sigh. "Such an amazingly tiring exercise it is to be got up for such outings."

"But, Mama, we are already late," Nell pointed out. "Lord Warwynne will be wondering what has become of us."

"Oh, you need not worry, Miss Trant," Sir Charles put in smoothly. "The young pup will stay to bark at your heels."

Turning a cool shoulder to him, Nell faced her mother, who had settled into the jade cushion of a japanned settee and shut her eyes. "I really must insist that we set out, Mama. We should not abuse the viscount's generosity in this shameful manner."

The heavy lids rose slowly, but her mother stayed in her seat. "Has the carriage been brought round?"

"Long ago," Nell replied with a touch of asperity.

The eyes closed. Then a deep rumbling sigh was heard and Mama put out a hand. "Sir Charles, if you please."

The baronet stepped promptly forward and helped Mrs. Trant to her feet. Mr. Perkins was left to offer his arm to both young ladies, and, as Nell laid her hand on his sleeve, she seethed with impotent rage. Lord Warwynne might indeed be a mere pup, but at least he was a gentleman. And one, what is more, who valued her quite for herself. He was neither dissolute nor a rake. He was perhaps somewhat too earnest, but that was merely a youthful failing. He was, in fact, a veritable paragon, and she was a fool.

During the journey to the theater in Sir Charles's elegant lozenged town coach, Nell berated herself for not having the good sense to care the least bit for Viscount Warwynne. His lordship had been as attentive to her this past week as only a young man in love can be, yet to her it had meant only a chance to briefly escape the turmoil of her emotions. For all her thoughts of market marriages, Eleanor had no real intention of making one for herself. Such a match was repugnant to her very nature. Was this not why she objected to Beth's betrothment? As she stepped from the carriage with the aid of an ornately liveried footman, she consoled herself with the thought that for Lord Warwynne it was but a calf-love, an infatuation he would soon forget.

They entered the theater in a grand procession behind Eugenia Trant's regal train to discover Lord Warwynne standing dismally by the sweeping staircase, a bouquet of roses drooping in one hand. His fair head might have been bowed in melancholy reflection had not the exessively high points of his collar impeded such an action. But the slump of the shoulders encased in an elegant plum evening coat and the sag of the once-starched cravat told them all of his lordship's despondency. Catching sight of Miss Trant, however, Lord Warwynne underwent an amazing transformation, his figure springing to life as he dashed forward with an eager smile and anxious words.

"Oh, Miss Trant! I was certain some misfortune had befallen you—that you would not come—that—" Suddenly he seemed to recall the others surrounding them and broke off in confusion. Flushing brightly, he brushed back his thin blond hair and made a deep bow. "Mrs. Trant, ma'am, Miss Elizabeth, gentlemen."

But it was obvious that only Miss Eleanor Trant existed for him. He presented her grandly with the bouquet and his arm at one and the same time and, though she thanked him prettily enough, Nell ascended the stairs with a plummeting heart. Too many of the baronet's thrusts had gone home for her to ignore the boy's increasingly effusive infatuation, but she did not have time to consider precisely what she should do before they reached his lordship's gilded box.

"Now, Mama, I think you should sit up front with Sir Charles next to you, whilst Lord Warwynne and I take the seats to the left. Mr. Perkins and Beth will not object to having the seats behind, I'm sure," Nell directed as they passed through the curtains into the box.

Several eyes focused on the latecomers, but none hushed them as it was only the one-act in progress, to which no one was paying the least attention. Through the theater, a babble rose and fell like the tides of the sea, and a number of acquaintances called out to them from both the pit and boxes across the way. With a royally languid nod, Mrs. Trant acknowledged a select few, then descended in a swaying rustle of satin onto the velvet chair.

The others remained standing as Mr. Perkins voiced a

whispered objection to Nell's plans. "But of course Miss Elizabeth must be seated next to Sir Charles," he was saying to a stony-faced Miss Trant. "I shall be happy—no, honored—to take the chair beside your mother."

"But I assure you, Mr. Perkins—" Nell began, only to be cut off by an impatient Lord Warwynne.

"It surely does not matter where *they* sit, Miss Trant, so long as *you* are beside me," he insisted reverently as he drew her reluctantly to the chair next to his.

Frustrated, but unable to continue her protests, Nell sat down rather forcefully, a tight smile fixed on her face for the benefit of any curious onlookers. Mr. Perkins was, in her view, positively *stuffy!* If he lost Beth to the baronet, it would be no less than what he deserved! A man who would not make the least attempt to procure the hand of the woman he loved had absolutely no right to love at all.

Suddenly Nell became aware of a strange warmth covering her hand and looked down to discover Lord Warwynne's white glove placed upon hers. With an ungentle yank, Nell recovered possession of her hand and delivered a fulminating glare to the unfortunate viscount. His lordship's face fell comically. He instantly turned crimson in contrition, and Nell knew a moment of pity mingled with self-recrimination. She leaned toward him and playfully rapped his knuckles with her fan, then graced him with an encouraging smile to let him know she was not truly angry. His flush faded from his narrow face, and he looked at her with the eyes of a grateful puppy. Conscience-smitten, Nell turned her attention to the action on the stage below.

Viscount Warwynne's party remained in their seats at the end of the one-act and received visitors in his box. The theater hummed and buzzed noisily with little time for any action on Nell's part, though she did attempt a whispered aside to Mr. Perkins that Beth might wish to take a brief airing. He reacted with stiff pride, telling her in a stern hiss that any suggestion of impropriety on his part toward a woman about to be affianced to another man would simply not do.

Nell ground her teeth audibly, though no one could hear over the babble in the small box. Catching sight of Sir Charles, however, Nell had the uncomfortable conviction that he was somehow aware of her maneuverings, and she instantly felt a spurt of resentment toward the man who was, after all, the source of all her troubles. During the first act of the Shakespearean tragedy—she was not even certain which one it was, so befuddled by her own woes was she—Nell felt his burning stare upon her. Somewhat grateful that he was behind her and could not actually see the discomfiture she was suffering, she nonetheless could not shake the disturbing notion that the baronet knew precisely what she was thinking and feeling.

As the curtain fell on what to Eleanor had seemed an endless piece of gibberish, everyone stood as if by previous agreement. Mr. Perkins departed to procure a glass of lemonade for Mama—who, of course, had been the only one to remain seated—while Beth stepped into the passageway on Sir Charles's arm. Gritting her teeth, Nell accepted Lord Warwynne's offer of escort and they, too, entered the corridor, which was rapidly filling with befrilled, bejeweled and bedaubed members of London's *haut ton*.

Absolutely nothing was going as Nell had planned. How would she ever contrive to settle things between Beth and Mr. Perkins if they did not *cooperate?* Really, she was quite put out with them both! She did not know precisely how or why, but she was certain tonight's failure was Sir Charles's doing, and she experienced a resurgence of her hostility toward him.

A flash of light caught her eye as Lord Warwynne flipped open an ornate diamond-encrusted snuffbox. A speculative gleam came into Nell's eye and she tapped his sleeve lightly.

"Do you think we could be alone a moment, my lord? I should like to . . . to speak with you about a very important matter."

His lordship looked at her as if he had just been given the key to heaven. "Of course, of course." He nodded vigorously.

They had stopped before the draped entrance to another box. Warwynne now split the curtains, looked inside, then with his hand on her elbow, he guided her within. The box was deserted. They stood hidden from view in the darkest shadows at the very back.

"Now tell me what I may do for you," he said.

Nell firmly stifled any doubts about the wisdom of her actions and parted her lips in a smile that had an instant effect on the viscount. He gulped as she spoke.

"This is, my lord, a matter of some...delicacy," Nell began. She halted abruptly. His lordship's eyes had a heated glow that was very different from their usual friendly warmth.

"I beg you will call me Arthur," he said with a strange urgency.

"Very well, if you wish, Arthur," she agreed, biting her lip, her doubts mushrooming. Suddenly she changed her mind. "I think we should perhaps return to our box."

The viscount leaned forward until his thigh pressed against her thin muslin dress and his warm breath sent the loose wisps of her hair fluttering at her neck. "There—there is something I must tell you! I cannot wait any longer! I seem to have waited for *years* already!"

Like an iron weight, sudden dread oppressed Nell, making her forget the rebuff she had been about to make. "W-what is that?" she asked tremulously, not wishing to receive an answer.

"My dear, dear Miss Trant," he exclaimed in a voice of ecstatic intoxication as he folded his arms about her. "Your hair is like—is like the setting sun! Your eyes are the most precious of gems! Your lips—your lips are—"

"Lord Warwynne! What are you saying?" Nell cut in with acute distress. She tried to escape his bumbling embrace, but her resistance only seemed to increase his lordship's ardor.

Fondling her bare shoulders with eager hands and nuzzling his lips into the crown of her hair, he groaned, then replied rapturously, "Oh, Miss Trant—Eleanor—my love! I am asking you to be my wife!"

Nell was so astonished that she ceased to struggle altogether and meekly accepted the kiss he planted on her cheek. "Your *wife?*" she echoed blankly.

"My dearest! My Eleanor! Tell me you will be mine!"

His hands began to slide downward, the sticky heat of his breath clung to her neck, and his body strained more tightly against hers, shaking her violently from her stupor. Raising her hands, Nell freed herself from his grasp with a hard thrust upon his shoulders.

"My lord, you forget yourself," she hissed on a shaky breath. "I have not given you permission to use my name, nor to—to address me in this manner. There is not the least possibility of an alliance between us."

His narrow face whitened, then went as scarlet as the velvet seats. "But my dear—my—Miss Trant," he stuttered. "You—you must! You *must* be mine! I love you!"

She flinched to hear the words spoken with such heated desire. Catching her off guard, he again encaptured her in a clumsy embrace and endeavored to smother her lips with his. As Nell twisted her head rapidly, he was unable to succeed, but he left a hot, moist imprint along her cheek that left her feeling sick. She had closed her eyes to shut out the sight of his flushed fervor and opened her mouth to utter a violent protest when she was released abruptly. Her eyes flew open to behold Viscount Warwynne dangling in the furious grip of a wrathful Sir Charles.

"I believe," Grayson remarked with tight control, "that the lady does not wish for your addresses, my lord. I suggest that you cease to importune upon her further."

He dropped the viscount to his feet as carelessly as one might release a kerchief to float to the ground, then took Nell's hand in a crushing grip. "Come, Miss Trant, it is time you returned to your seat."

There was no mistaking the rage ripping in each word, but Nell allowed herself to be dragged from the box with a sense of relief. She had never anticipated such a scene, and the entire episode had been keenly distressful. She was not, however, prepared for the baronet's vehemence. Clamping her upper arm with a clasp as tight as a slaveband, he yanked her behind a fluted colonnade and glared down at her with eyes of blazing fury.

"I trust you now realize, Miss Trant, just what happens when you encourage a calfling like Warwynne," he rasped at her through tight lips. "A mutton-headed gapeseed would have predicted the outcome of your flirtatious behavior all this past week."

All of Nell's gratitude fled before this assault. Her back stiffened, and she tilted her nose defiantly. *"You,* sir, do not have the right to pass judgment on my behavior. Furthermore, I was not *flirting!"*

"I should like to know what you call brazen coquetry if not flirtation, ma'am! That pup cannot be blamed for thinking you *fast,* given your hoydenish manner. I take leave to warn you that if you continue in such bold ways, you shall acquire a reputation as another Caro Lamb."

Her mouth worked soundlessly and her breasts strained against the bodice of her dress as she angrily gulped in air. At last, in a voice of fierce resentment, Nell informed Sir Charles that she did not have to listen to his quite uncalled-for sermonizing another instant. She wrenched her arm free and took one agitated step, only to be jerked back behind the colonnade.

"I suggest, ma'am," he ground out, "that you make some attempt to straighten your hair. Your feathers have nearly been plucked, my dear," he added in unmistakable mockery, "and unless you wish for the world to know of your love-making—"

"Oh!" she gasped. "I have *not* been—"

"—you will endeavor to restore them to their former glory," he finished tautly.

With hands that shook Nell complied with his order while Sir Charles continued to shield her from the eyes of passersby. Though the exchange of inflamed whispers had taken mere seconds, it had seemed endless to her, and she longed only to be away from his infuriating presence. She yearned to go directly home, yet she knew such an abrupt departure would occasion the very talk she most wished to prevent.

The instant that her plumes were repositioned to some semblance of order, Sir Charles turned and led her back to the box. Though not another word passed between them, Nell knew that her escort was laboring under an acute anger. She felt his leashed tension in every step he took. Shame pricked her deeply, for she knew his disapprobation was fully justified. Deep inside she felt profoundly grateful to the baronet, both for his timely rescue and for his aid in forestalling any scandalous gossip. But Nell's galling humiliation could only find release in violent animosity toward her benefactor.

How dare he? she thought over and over until the words hammered in her head as white-hot as molten iron on a smithy's anvil. How dare he lecture to me? If she were a man she would have planted him a facer—or whatever it was men did when insulted. Her good sense was thoroughly overcome by her intense desire to show Sir Charles that she would not permit him to dictate her behavior.

Upon reentering their box, Nell took her seat and began chattering with false animation to Mr. Perkins on her right. Lord Warwynne was nowhere to be seen and, though both Mama and Beth looked at Nell inquiringly, no one gave voice to the unspoken question. Just as the curtain rose on the second act, his lordship slipped into his seat at Nell's left, but she kept her shoulder turned slightly away from him, fixing her attention firmly on the stage below.

At the second intermission, intent upon avoiding both the viscount and the baronet, Nell moved quickly to take Mr. Perkins's sleeve.

"The box is rather stuffy, you know," she said as she waved her fan vigorously.

It strained all her powers of dissimulation, but Nell produced at least a semblance of animation in Mr. Perkins's company. Meeting the sneering disapproval in Sir Charles's sapphire gaze, she called upon all her feminine wiles and, in a dazzling performance far superior to anything on the stage below, she exhibited a marked degree of partiality for the bewildered gentleman. Uncomfortable and uncertain what to do in the face of this unexpected attention, Mr. Perkins nonetheless responded with civility to Nell's demands. By the end of the evening the viscount was sulking in dejected injury while Beth sank into distressed misery. But the silent, vibrant condemnation oozing from Sir Charles goaded Nell the most, bringing a flashing sparkle to her eyes and a flirtatious smile to her lips as she devoted herself to Mr. Perkins.

## - 9 -

STARING OUT A rain-spattered window at a dreary sky as leaden as her spirits, Nell had not, at first, heard Beth's softly spoken comments. Jerkily, as if pulled unwillingly back to the reality of the breakfast room, she faced her sister across the table.

"I'm sorry. Did you say something?"

"I—well, I," Beth began tentatively, lines of distress etched beside her mouth. "I remarked upon your behavior last evening."

The teacup traveling to Nell's lips paused in midair. "Oh?"

This short, sharp inquiry knocked the breath from her sister. Her eyes studiously watched her fingers work a knot into the lace ruffling on her rose-striped round gown as she ventured timorously, "It—I—you did not behave—well, at all *seemly*, my dear."

Though she knew it was the truth, Nell was not prepared to hear it. The events of the night before had already exacerbated her beyond the limits of common sense, and she now flared into an irrational defense of her behavior.

"And just what, may I ask, does that mean?" Nell snapped, returning her flowered china cup to its saucer with a ringing crash. "Am I to take it that you have been listening to Sir Charles's censorious views of my behavior?"

"Sir Charles?" Beth repeated, eyeing the cup as if she expected to discover it now split in two. "I don't know what *his* views may be, but you must know, Nell, that your actions last night were not quite the thing."

"I am sorry, Elizabeth, but I do not know such a thing at all!" her sister harshly dissented through clenched teeth. "In fact, I believe I behaved as seemly as anyone else and do not understand why you must needs lecture me on a subject which is, after all, not the least of your concern."

Though her color drained from her face at this rebuke, Beth straightened in her chair and thrust her round chin into the air. "But of course it is my concern, Nell. You are my sister and your actions reflect upon the whole family."

"Oh, I see!" Nell exclaimed, flinging back her chair as she jumped up in a flurry of dark blue. From the coils of her loose ringlets to the plain hem of her unadorned navy gown, she was a narrow line of inflexible fury. "It is not truly my behavior that concerns you, but only the good of the *family!* Well, I might point out that you fret needlessly, my dear sister. Nothing I shall do could possibly reflect upon the family any more poorly than your alliance with a notorious rake!"

"Oh!" Beth cried, stung out of her usual timidity. She rose to meet her sister's angry taunts head-on. "If you wish to cast names upon people, Eleanor, I take leave to tell you that you are nothing but an outrageous *flirt!* I can only say that I am ashamed to call you my sister."

Beth whirled and ran from the breakfast room before Nell could reply to this intolerable calumny. The door shivered shut on the younger woman's hostile retreat, followed by a splintering clatter as Nell hurled her half-full cup against the closing wood.

Trembling from head to foot, Nell was at first unable to move. Never before had she and Beth engaged in anything more serious than the merest spat. She thought for a moment that she must still be locked in one of the horrendous nightmares that had not permitted her to rest throughout the long night, but her gaze slowly traced the stain that splayed over the wood door to run in streams to the shattered remains of the porcelain cup, and she knew it had been no dream, no nightmare from which she could wake with relief. It had been real enough, and Nell felt instant remorse that she could so lose control of her temper with Beth.

Wrenching open the door, she mounted the stairs in twos, her long skirt hiked indecorously above her knees. She was about to climb to the upper floor, certain Beth would have sought the refuge of her bedchamber, when a muffled sound from the morning room arrested her. Turning swiftly, she entered without knocking, words of apology already spilling from her lips.

Enfolded into his greatcoat, her sobs suppressed by the damp capes at his shoulder, Beth stood within the comforting circle of Sir Charles's arms. Nell's pleas for forgiveness died on her lips as she took in the intimacy of their embrace. Like the china cup, her heart dashed into a multitude of splinters, each piercing her with pricks of pain until her aching was magnified beyond bearing. She would have backed out without another word, but they both turned to look at her, disengaging themselves with embarrassment.

"Forgive me," Nell said in a midwinter voice. "I did not know you were using this room for your *lovemaking.*"

With a swish of her skirt and a slam of the door, she left before they could respond. Thus, her apology was neither made nor accepted. Had Nell been granted a period of quiet reflection, it is possible she would have yet overruled her pride and returned to beg her sister's forgiveness. But she left the morning room, she encountered Fowles, who stopped her to present her with a gilt-edged card.

Glancing at it with a stormy impatience, Nell found it to be from Viscount Warwynne.

"His lordship begs a word with you, miss," said the Friday-faced servant.

She was tempted to deny the viscount, but she knew she had been grieviously at fault with him. Not one to shirk an unpleasant responsibility, she nodded and instructed Fowles to show his lordship into the formal sitting room. Running her fingers through her tangled curls, then tugging her lace fichu into place about her neck, Nell sought the strength to endure this unsought interview as she took a seat facing the door. The viscount entered wearing a face of abject remorse and for one terrifying moment, Nell thought he was going to throw himself on his knees before her.

"Please sit down, Lord Warwynne," she said quickly,

gesturing to the lyre-back chair opposite the settee on which she sat. To her great relief, after an indecisive wavering, the viscount took the seat indicated, nervously brushed his hair back from his pale brow, and cleared his throat noisily.

"My dear Miss Trant," he began as if reciting a learned piece, "I come to request your forgiveness for my appalling behavior toward yourself last evening and to—"

"Of course I forgive you," Nell cut in. She leaned forward and added earnestly, "It was as much as my fault as yours, my lord, and I ask *you* to forgive *me*. I should never have led you to believe, to expect that I would welcome—"

"You need not apologize for *your* behavior," he interrupted with feeling. "I know full well I went beyond the pale. I should never have been so lost to all sense as to— as to take advantage as I did."

Staring at the stains of color on his thin cheeks, Nell felt another wave of guilty regret for her actions. "We shall forget the matter, my lord," she said firmly.

His lordship's relief was evident in the gratitude flooding his flushed face. He dug his toe into the carpet and examined the flowered pattern on the corner screen as if seeking the answer to divine truth in the colored silk. Finally he cleared his throat and managed, "Does this mean . . . could you possibly consider . . . will you marry me?"

Nell smothered her impulse to laugh and strove to remember the proper etiquette. At last she produced in an almost calm voice, "I am honored, of course, my lord, but I can never accept your generous offer."

"But why not?" the viscount queried with a hint of a sulk.

"Well, for one thing, you are younger than I am. Though a lady does not generally like to admit such a thing, I shall confess, my lord, that I am approaching four-and-twenty," Nell explained. When he began to protest, she raised a slim hand to silence him. "Don't try to hoax me, my lord, into believing that you are any older than one-and-twenty because I shan't accept it as the truth."

Red-faced and with a sheepish smile, his lordship reluctantly admitted his youth. "But I do not see that it is such a vast difference of age, Miss Trant. And I shall grow older, you know."

She smiled but said firmly, "But so, my lord, shall I. Further, I'm afraid I do not have, nor do I believe myself capable of ever having, the finer feeling that must exist between a man and woman who wish to wed. Let us forget all this foolishness—both mine and yours—and agree to remain friends."

The young man studied the buttons on his yellow kid gloves, the turndown cuffs on his black high-top boots, and the barely discernible pattern on the old rug, then finally raised his puppy-brown eyes to her face. He nodded briefly, sending his blond hair straying over his brow again. "I shall be happy to remain your friend, Miss Trant, though I devoutly wish I could be more."

Nell shook her head. "You have much to see of the world yet, my lord, and no doubt one day you will thank me for having had the sense to pass by all that you are offering me."

He seemed inclined to protest this point, but was persuaded at last to cease voicing his objections. After a stretch of silence and just as Nell was about to bid him good day, Warwynne suddenly inquired, "What was it you wished to speak privately to me about last night?"

Nell paused, uncertain now whether to confide in him. Then her eyes swam with a moist memory of the intimate embrace she had so recently witnessed, and she said rather brusquely, "I am in need of a sum of money, my lord. Rather a large sum, and I thought perhaps you might help me."

He looked eager. "Of course! How much of the blunt d'you need, Miss Trant?"

"Twenty thousand pounds."

His mouth dropped open and worked mutely. In the end all he managed was a soundless whistle. The hope that had flared to life within Nell flickered a moment more, then died.

"You have not got such a sum?" she asked flatly.

"Well . . . no," his lordship admitted. Watching the defeat cross her face, he added warmly, "I should be happy to lend you what I can. As soon as I get my next quarter's allowance, I'll have plenty of the ready."

Brightening slightly, Nell asked, "And when is that?"

"At the end of June."

Her face fell again like water over a fall. "Oh. That shall be much, much too late. But thank you for your kind offer."

At length he departed on the assurance that she would not hesitate to call upon him if he might be of any help to her. The door had scarcely closed upon his heels when it was thrust suddenly open once again. Nell looked up to find herself the object of a searing examination by a clearly vexed baronet.

"Still trying to leash your puppy, are you, Miss Trant?" Sir Charles inquired jeeringly as he kicked the door closed with the back of a tassled hessian. "Do you think you can keep him to heel these days?"

He had discarded his greatcoat, and she could not help but notice his muscles rippling beneath his tight dove-gray pantaloons as he crossed the room with long, angry strides. Embarrassed that she should observe such a thing, her eyes flew back up to his face; then instantly she wished she had looked anywhere else but into his steely gaze. His eyes raked over her with scorn as he stood before her, his hands planted on his narrow hips with little regard for the cut of his taupe morning coat. His gaze clearly bespoke his contempt for what he saw.

Maddeningly, Nell felt herself slowly flush under his intense probe. Then once again she vividly recalled the sight of his arms wrapped about Elizabeth, and her figure stiffened as she glared steadily back at him. But her eyes fell first, reaching the intricate knot of his black cravat before she requested, "You wanted something of me, sir?"

"What I want of you, Miss Trant, would likely find me swinging from a Tyburn collar!" Sir Charles responded sharply. "But as I have little wish to be hanged, I shall restrict myself to informing you that you are not to ever again overset Beth. I've come to expect that devilish temper of yours, but she has yet to learn how to protect herself against your stinging tongue. I'll not have you playing hell with her, sending her into such a pucker simply because you cannot find another unfortunate on whom to loosen your venom. If you cannot refrain from these distempered freaks, then I suggest you return to Norfolk with the next post."

During this raging assault, Nell went from flaming red to spectral white. She now stared at Sir Charles with wide eyes in a ghostly face as varied emotions battled within her.

Uppermost was her own shame over what she acknowledged to be just accusations. But a mixture of injured pride and furious resentment of his criticisms kept her from openly admitting, as she truly desired to do, that she was indeed utterly at fault and grievously sorry for the argument with Beth. Thus, when his hands dropped and he goaded her with an annihilating elevation of his brow, accompanied with a frozen "Well?," she rose from her seat with wounded dignity.

"I believe, sir, you are referring to matters that are of concern only to my sister and me," she stated firmly.

"Need I remind you, ma'am, that Miss Beth is to become my wife?" he pointed out flatly. "It is my obligation to protect her."

"Beth stands in no need of protection from me," Nell returned, inwardly wincing even as she made this denial.

With a withering sneer Sir Charles continued, "Protection from your venom is precisely what she *does* need, Miss Trant. You of all people should know she cannot bear such cruelty as you cast upon her this morning. If you should so overset her again, ma'am, I shall personally set you upon the stage to Norwich."

"Are you threatening me, Sir Charles?" Nell queried stiffly.

"Let us say I am informing you of the consequences of your actions."

Her lips tightened into an almost invisible line. Though she knew she deserved this dressing-down, it did not hurt the less to receive it. And she thought would surely die from the ache within her at his expression of scorn, pity, and dislike. Suddenly she could not bear such looks an instant longer. Her heart had been broken long ago, but it was breaking again. She had heard it shatter when she saw Beth in his arms, and now she felt the pang as he crushed the shards to dust beneath his censorious aversion.

Wanting only to get away from the misery, from the heartache she did not wish to examine, Nell blindly put out a trembling hand. She turned and moved mechanically toward the door, not seeing, not hearing. Thus, it came as a surprise to feel herself held back, to feel his arms engulf her thin figure, to hear his voice in a stream above her ear. Dully, she became aware of the words within the sound and listened for a disbelieving moment before pushing his arms away.

"I—I do not need *you* to tell me when to apologize to my sister," she said unsteadily, gazing steadfastly at the third mother-of-pearl button on his cream waistcoat. "Nor do I need you to involve yourself with any of my affairs."

He subjected her to another harsh scrutiny from those hard eyes, then moved to flick a lazy finger against her pale cheek. "I see. You now feel yourself perfectly capable of controlling your young pup. Are you as certain of Mr. Perkins?"

"Mr. Perkins is a *gentleman*," Nell retorted.

"Ah," he drawled in a voice that made her fingers curl up into her palms. "Well, my dear, I am certain you know best what you want, and if it is a reputation as a hoyden, who am I to say you nay?"

Her eyes flashed with warning as they swept up to his. "Thank you, sir! You have made your opinion of me quite plain, and I shouldn't dream of inflicting my *hoydenish* presence upon you a moment longer."

Again she turned to the door, her hand on the brass knob, but his palm forced the wood closed, and as she turned an infuriated face up to him, he said on a note of command, "I will have your word, Miss Trant, that you will leave Beth out of your embittered battle with the rest of the world. You may save your arrows to sling at me, if you wish, or possibly one of your beaux has become fond of that shrew's tongue you own, but I warn you, I will not tolerate your abuse of that child."

*"You* will not tolerate," Nell repeated, her voice as numb as her feelings. She stared at the hand pressing against the dark wood of the door, at the frills of the fine cambric shirt gracing the wrist, and felt as if a saber had been thrust through her middle. Her unbound copper hair shook with an emphatic nod. "I see. I assure you, Sir Charles, that *you* need not concern yourself with me again."

Still the hand did not move. Her eyes inched reluctantly beyond the frilled cuff, up the taupe sleeve, past the broad shoulder to his shuttered face. For what seemed to Nell like an eternal descent into hellfire, they gazed wordlessly at one another. Then the baronet straightened, his hand fell away, she threw open the door, and escaped from his burning hostility.

Nell flew through her room in a frenzied whirl. She jerked two portmanteaux from the top of her wardrobe, pitched them open onto the floor, and began to dash wildly forward and backward. From wardrobe to vanity, from vanity to wardrobe, she grasped without seeing to fling dresses, shawls, shoes, brushes, books, ribbons—everything, in short, she could lay hands on—into the boxes. She did not shriek or cry out as her soul longed to do, but crossed her room in a tight-lipped, frantic silence.

He wanted her gone. Very well, she would leave! This moment! She would not inflict her presence on him, on Beth, on anyone a moment longer! These thoughts bludgeoned themselves repeatedly against her head until it ached as even her heart ached. Still she scrambled in a race against her own tortuous misery, stumbling into the growing litter on her floor to sling down yet another dress, another glove.

At the end of thirty crazed minutes of distracted snatching and hurling, blind seizing and tossing, Nell's foot caught on the hem of a discarded pelisse, rending the cloth and sending her sprawling to the floor in one ungainly motion. As she collapsed beside the entangled jumble heaped in colorful disarray, she burst into sobs. Her body twisted with sorrow and she cried as though she had saved all the tears of a lifetime for this moment.

When at last her wrenching tears became hiccups, Nell straightened, wiped her face with the flounce of a lemon poplin dress, and tried to regain control of herself. She forced herself to face what had just occurred.

What was happening to her? What had become of the cool, calm headmistress of Trant's Establishment for Young Ladies? She looked sadly at the disheveled hodgepodge strewn haphazardly about her and thought the picture an apt description of her mind—a muddled farrago of varied nonsense. Without wishing to, Nell recognized the reason for her disordered mental state, and tears trickled down her cheeks anew. Above all, she did not wish to admit what she could no longer deny, even to herself.

All those years, all those miles away from her memories, it had been easy to pretend. She had nearly convinced herself, too, that she no longer cared. But the pretense was over. Her love for Sir Charles Grayson flamed more hotly than ever before, and it was reducing her to ashes.

She wrapped her arms around her and, hugging herself as if to squeeze out all the renewed pain, Nell began to examine her actions over the past weeks. She had, she now acknowledged, objected to Beth's betrothment from jealousy—ugly, undeniable jealousy. She had no right to oppose the match. She would bury her feelings and accept it as she must. And she would return to Norfolk as soon as possible.

Casting her eyes over the tumbled clutter she had created, the ghost of a smile graced her mournful lips. She could not, of course, leave as quickly as she had intended an hour ago. An abrupt departure would occasion just the sort of talk she most desired to avoid. But at the end of a week she would be on the stage for Norfolk, and she would allow no one to talk her out of it. The baronet wished expressly for her to be gone, she thought with a sharp pang, and so, more than anything, did she!

# - 10 -

As WILL OFTEN happen in the spring, the days had gone unexpectedly from brisk to balmy. Thus the newly repaired hem of Nell's pelisse lay over the banded portmanteaux in the hall while only a light cashmere shawl draped her shoulders. She had knotted her hair tightly at the nape of her neck, as befit a headmistress, and covered it with an unassuming cloth bonnet of the same dull brown as her sensible traveling gown. She pulled on her gloves with short, efficient snaps and bid Fowles good-bye without revealing a hint of the sadness she was feeling.

Indeed, as she checked within the depths of her fringed silk reticule to once again count the funds for her journey, Nell wondered if she would ever feel happy again. Certainly she had not known a moment's peace over the past week. Though she had wanted to time and again, she had never reconciled with Beth and thus, a keen remorse had been added to her inner distress and had strengthened the stiff reserve with which she treated everyone. Coldest of all was her treatment of Sir Charles, to whom she had scarcely spoken since he had made so clear his desire to see her gone.

She had had, moreover, another battle with her mother, who seemed to take Nell's departure as a personal insult.

This time, however, Nell had remained staunch. She must return to Norfolk and no amount of arguing could change her mind. Her leavetaking had been brief and chilled. Mama was not, it seemed, prepared to forgive her. Nell sighed and cast one last look about the hall, told herself she must be catching cold, so watery had her eyes become, and headed for the door.

A rustle of skirts and patter of feet halted her. Looking over her shoulder, she saw Beth flying down the staircase the instant before she was captured in the young girl's arms. The Trant sisters exchanged a fervent embrace.

"Oh, Nell, I am so very *sorry!*" cried Beth. "Do you think you can forgive me enough to stay?"

Relief flooded Nell, and she held on tightly for a long moment before detaching Beth with a laugh. "Don't be a silly goose, dearest! It is *I* who must ask your forgiveness! You cannot think I am leaving because of you. It is simply time for me to get back to my duties. I've a school to run, you know. I cannot neglect it any longer."

"Are you certain you cannot stay?" Beth pleaded, her blue eyes sorrowful in her round face. "Not even for my ball? It's but two weeks away."

"Yes, I'm certain," Nell answered firmly. Then, as Elizabeth showed a distressing tendency to shed tears, Nell added briskly, "You don't need me to enjoy your ball. All the preparations are in order. All you and Mama need do is present yourselves in your prettiest gowns and enjoy the evening. And Beth—I am sorry. I never meant to lose my temper with *you.*"

Impulsively, she scooped Beth back into the circle of her arms for a tight hug. Fowles's discreet cough parted them. Together they laughed with embarrassment, then Nell gathered herself together with a show of festive anticipation for her journey and once again moved to leave.

A series of raps startled them. Fowles, who had carried the portmanteaux to the door, was shaken from his usual poise. Recovering, he dropped the boxes to the floor with a clatter and hastened to admit the newcomer.

"This must be my hack," Nell was saying with a lopsided smile that twisted further still when she looked up to behold Sir Charles. Her pulse raced. She had not thought to see him again. For one brief instant, she allowed herself the joy of seeing his handsome features one last time.

A strange glitter shone his azure eyes, and his black curls were more disheveled than ever, but there was nothing novel about the mocking curve upon his chiseled lips, which dropped kisses or jibes with the same careless ease. Flushing, Nell instantly busied herself with readjusting the set of her shawl. Her spine was as rigid as granite when he spoke.

"Hack indeed, Miss Trant. I've come to take you to Lombard Street." Nell's eyes narrowed as she noticed the slight sway to his stance, and the barely perceptive slur of his words.

"Oh, how kind, Sir Charles!" Beth exclaimed, wiping away a last tear. "Is it not kind of him, Nell, to take you to catch your coach?"

"Yes, kind," Nell agreed in the tone of one who disagrees violently but is too polite to say so. "In fact, Sir Charles need not be so kind. I've already summoned a hack."

"So unsummon the hack," he said with a shrug and a charmingly crooked grin.

Immediately, Nell's head swung up and she looked directly at him, her emerald eyes narrowed further against the glimmer of his sapphire gaze. His grin widened, he winked, and she stared at him astounded.

"Why, you've been *drinking!*" she accused.

He bowed. "Preparing for this moment, m'dear."

"I will not," she stated with resolution, "ride anywhere with a man who is *foxed.*"

"But I object, m'dear, to the term 'foxed.' I may be a little cut over the head, but foxed—no, I assure you." He leaned back against the wall, shoved his hands into the pockets of his claret morning coat, and smiled at her.

Nell turned away. For some reason both the smile and the glint in his eyes had become menacing. She felt the blood pounding in her temples and knew she must not be alone with him. Once alone, sense and propriety would lose all meaning. She felt weak with desire at the mere thought. Calling upon her resolve, she repeated firmly, "I cannot possibly accept your kind offer, Sir Charles."

"But I insist."

She rounded on him then, about to make a heated protest, but a sharp knock on the door prevented her. As Fowles moved to answer it, she contented herself with saying,

"There you see, my hack has arrived. Thank you for your offer, Sir Charles. Good-bye, dear Beth."

The baronet moved quickly to stand in front of her. Thus she was forced to look over his wide shoulder to view the door, and her mouth gaped open as Drusilla Poole entered the crowded hall. Sir Charles turned to see her and swore softly.

A bandbox in one hand and a cloth valise in the other, the spare, somewhat severe figure of Miss Poole marched toward Nell. Lines engraved beside a wide mouth that seemed never to have smiled, eyes that drooped at the corners and a nose that was definitely hooked at the end—these composed the long face of a woman who plainly disapproved of what she saw. Dressed in a cloak and gown more practical than fashionable, with every fading strand of hair coiled immaculately in place, she looked like an Amazon striding into battle. She cast not even the smallest glance at the gentleman now standing at Nell's shoulder and greeted her friend with a bob of her head.

"Drusilla! W-what are you doing here?" Nell managed weakly in response.

"Why, I told you I would come," Miss Poole answered. "Good day, Sir Charles," she added with a short nod, for all the world as if it had been just yesterday and not a disastrous evening more than three years ago since they had last met.

Perhaps, in other circumstances, Sir Charles would have replied in kind, would have kept up the polite facade. But now he threw back his handsome head and laughed, a jeering laugh that disquieted Nell. "It's hell's own jest, Nell, m'dear," he cried.

The three women all looked at him as if he were demented, while Fowles announced the arrival, at long last, of Nell's hackney coach. Then, as though prisoners set free, a trio of voices rose at once.

"I'm afraid we do not see the joke, Sir Charles," Nell said severely.

"A hackney? But why, my dear?" Miss Poole inquired of Miss Trant.

"Do you think Sir Charles would benefit from one of Papa's restoratives, Nell?" Elizabeth asked, her worried eyes flitting from the baronet to her sister and back again.

Sir Charles continued to laugh, holding his sides and shaking his head as if helpless to stop. When Miss Poole pressed her wide mouth to form another question, Nell interrupted. "I was about to set out for Norfolk, Drusilla. I never meant to stay in London overlong. You knew that."

"But, my dear, you'd been gone so very long already. I closed the school a few weeks early and came to help you with the preparations you've undertaken for the family celebration." Miss Poole's dry, crisp voice managed to convey the magnitude of her sacrifice. Nell felt another twinge of guilt over forcing her friend to travel so far, so selflessly. She turned that guilt into anger.

"Will you kindly stop laughing?" she demanded of the baronet, stamping her small foot.

"Do you think the restorative?" Beth suggested fearfully yet again.

"Yes! No! I don't care!"

"What about the hackney, miss?" Fowles queried.

Before Nell could slay the servant with a few choice words, Miss Poole set down both her bags and neatly took control. "Send the hackney away, Fowles. We shan't need it now. Miss Elizabeth, procure the restorative, if you please, and bring it to us in the sitting room." As she spoke, she led both Nell and Sir Charles, one hand under an elbow of each, into that aforementioned room.

As they crossed the threshold, both her charges wrenched free and proceeded to opposite corners of the room. No longer laughing, the baronet flung himself onto a chair, cast one leg over the thin carved arm, and began to swing his boot lazily. Nell ripped her sensible bonnet from her head and dashed it to the floor. Miss Poole collected it as she passed by, lay it on a piecrust table behind her, and sat down sternly on the edge of the settee.

Stopping to stand before the unlit fireplace, Nell abruptly swung her booted foot and delivered a most unladylike kick to the logs. What was she to do? To go had been heartrending, but to stay would be far, far worse. To continue seeing him daily, speaking with him, would be intolerable! She chanced a quick glance at Sir Charles and felt a thundering of sheer annoyance at his carefree attitude.

He was disgusting, odious! To be foxed at this time of day! Really, it was no less than what she expected of the wretch. *Why* couldn't she hate him as she ought? *Why* did she feel this dreadful desire to further ruffle those disordered ebony locks, to darken the glitter of those vivid blue eyes? Shame sank heavily through her, weighting her with yet another burden of guilt. Ignoring Miss Poole's mildly murmured reproach, she tendered another violent assault upon the firelogs, then whirled to face the baronet.

"I do not see, sir, what you found so vastly amusing," she remarked harshly.

"Spiritous liquors will often have such an effect, I'm told," put in Miss Poole.

"It was not the brandy that amused me, ma'am," Sir Charles countered, his eyes following the movement of the golden tassel on his swaying boot.

"No? Then I pray you will inform us just what was so monstrously funny," Nell requested, her words filled with animosity.

"Why, I was laughing at the arrival of Miss Poole, of course," he replied.

Nell gasped and Miss Poole stiffened, raising a hand to stop Eleanor from speaking out. "Never mind, dear. I've always known the baronet disliked me excessively. Ah— here is Miss Elizabeth with something that should make the gentleman feel better."

"A large dose of manners is what he needs," Nell mumbled, vigorously stripping off her gloves and discarding them upon the mantel.

"Papa always says this makes him feel just the thing after a hard night," said Beth, handing a pewter mug to Sir Charles.

His lips curled up as he saluted Miss Poole with the mug, then downed the brew on a swallow. Grimacing, he returned the empty mug to Beth and demanded, "What the devil was that vile concoction?"

"Why, ale with lemon pressed into it and dashed with crushed red pepper. Papa says it clears his head."

"Lord, no wonder the man's got nothing but space left between his ears," Sir Charles responded cheerfully.

"There is no call for you to insult Mr. Trant, sir," Miss Poole reproved, stepping in before Nell had a chance. Continuing to use her best schoolmistress voice, she went on, "When you have had some time to reflect, I'm certain you will think better of such remarks."

"He never thinks better of such remarks!" Nell snapped. "And for you to admit to laughing at Miss Poole is infamous! But nothing less than what I've come to expect of you!"

The tasseled boot stopped in midair. "I am surprised, Miss Trant, that you did not see the humor in the situation. I had not thought you so dull-witted. At the instant of your rushing back to her, Miss Poole is come to you. Your mutual devotion would be affecting were it not so diverting."

The effect of this cynical revelation was profound. Elizabeth dropped the pewter mug with a crash, Miss Poole pursed her lips in severe disapprobation, and Nell stood, shaking and sputtering. "You, you, you—"

Nell never finished her epithet. One glance at her trembling figure was sufficient for Miss Poole, who rose, excused herself to the baronet, and hauled Nell from the room very like one of her schoolgirls caught in a misdeed. Once within the refuge of Nell's bedchamber, she granted Nell five minutes of stormy silence while she herself removed her gloves, hat and bonnet with the economy of motion she attached to each of her actions. Finally she placed herself directly in the path of Nell's impassioned pacing.

"Sit down, Eleanor. You are needlessly overwrought."

Looking at Drusilla for a moment as if she did not remember who she was, Nell at last gave herself a little shake, then dropped to the edge of her bed.

"You still love him," Miss Poole said in the same voice she had used when Miss Lydia Burnett, aged ten, was discovered eating a forbidden box of chocolates.

"I . . . yes," Nell admitted, her head bent.

"That is why you've lingered in Town."

"I . . . yes," she repeated sadly.

"I thought as much." Drusilla nodded. "That is why I have come to you."

"But there was no need. I was coming back. In fact, we must leave! We must go immediately!" Nell jumped up as if to dash for the door.

Miss Poole restrained her with a raised hand. "Nonsense! If you leave now, my dear, you will forever carry your . . . affection . . . for that man with you. You must stay to see him betrothed to your sister. Oh, it will be painful to you, I know, but if you see it to the end, my dear, it will help purge you of sentiments which are, after all, best forgotten."

"I . . . you . . . of course, Drusilla, you are right," Nell agreed wistfully. "I cannot imagine why I've been so utterly foolish."

"Well, I am here to stand you friend. Together we shall see this through."

"Oh, Dru! You are so good!" Nell cried, flinging herself into her friend's arms. This time her tears were gentle as they fell upon Miss Poole's bony shoulder. She tried hard to believe it was, indeed, best this way.

For the next several days, it appeared that Nell had accepted the fate life had cast for her. She threw herself wholeheartedly into making the final arrangements for Beth's ball, sharing all chores with Miss Poole. She and Sir Charles were forced to be together often, but as Nell was never without Drusilla beside her, she felt more than capable of meeting him with civility. It was as if there had never been a moment of feeling, caring, anger between them. And that, Nell told herself repeatedly, was precisely the way she wanted it.

Thus Nell's manner was almost gracious when Sir Charles was ushered into the morning room a week before the ball. He bent a stiff half-bow to Miss Poole, who received it without missing a stitch in her embroidery, then turned to face Nell, who was seated at the secretary.

"I've come to tell you, ma'am, that my mother has procured vouchers to Almack's. She bade me to request your presence there Wednesday evening."

"But how wonderful!" Nell exclaimed with a little clap of her hands. She rose from her chair and smiled at Sir Charles with unwonted warmth as she smoothed the creases from her sprigged muslin frock. "Of course we shall go. Please return our appreciation and acceptance to Lady Grayson. Oh, Drusilla, won't it be fun? Almack's! We shall have the most glorious time chaperoning Beth."

Flicking his kid gloves together, Sir Charles said with deliberation, "I regret to inform you, Miss Trant, that my mother was able to procure only two vouchers—one for Miss Elizabeth and one for yourself."

"Oh." The warmth drained from Nell's face, and the baronet's brows snapped together.

"It does not matter, dear," Miss Poole said placidly. "I fear I should not quite fit into the society at Almack's."

"Nonsense! Of course you'd fit in! Sir Charles, cannot Lady Grayson request a voucher for Miss Poole?"

His perfectly molded shoulders, encased in a well-tailored bottle-green coat, shrugged. "I believe not," he drawled in bored tones.

"But I am certain Lady Grayson—" Nell began. She looked directly into his eyes and instantly bristled at the harsh gleam she saw there. "You do not wish for her to go," she accused heatedly.

"You wrong me, Miss Trant. I most certainly wish for Miss Poole to go. But not, I admit, to Almack's."

"Oh! You! I could box your ears!" Nell exclaimed with vehemence.

Miss Poole set aside her stitchery and rose. "Do not fly into a taking, Eleanor. We both know that Sir Charles is being deliberately provoking."

"Ah, but the question is, have I provoked you, Miss Poole?" queried the baronet. He leveled his quizzing glass upon her, then sighed. "But of course not. How could I forget that you have no emotions to provoke?"

Nell's gasp was ignored. Miss Poole said simply, "I trust, Eleanor, that you will have the sense to accept Lady Grayson's generous offer. You must think of Miss Elizabeth, you know, dear."

"How thoughtful you are, Miss Poole," said Sir Charles. "Always thinking of others, aren't you?" The question ended on a sneer. Miss Poole stiffened.

Facing him without a twitch, she stated calmly, "I see you are in a difficult mood today, sir. I think perhaps you will not mind if I excuse myself. Do not linger, Eleanor," she ordered over her shoulder as she passed from the room.

Nell scarcely heard her. "How dare you!" she cried. "You have no right to insult my friends!" she declared as the door clapped shut behind them.

The sharp line of his mouth emphasized the uncompromising set of his jaw. His face, his stance, his very breath seemed taut with hostility. It came as a shock to hear his voice as smooth as silk.

"Well, my dear, does Saint George still get the prize for slaying the dragon?"

Her chest rose and fell heavily. "You, sir, are the farthest thing from a saint imaginable! If you will excuse me!"

"But I won't," he countered, moving more rapidly than she to block the path to the door.

Retreating a step from him, Nell said as scornfully as she could manage, "You may have the strength to keep me here, to make me listen to your abominable animadversions, but you cannot make me regard Miss Poole as anything other than a dear, good friend. She is worth dozens of you, sir!"

"So you have fully informed me, more times than I can count, my dear. Tell me, do you remain so loyal to every friend who ruins your life? Or was it her spiteful interference in what never concerned her that so endeared her to you?"

"You say these things because you know nothing of loyalty—or of fidelity!"

"I know that you allow Miss Poole to control you to an unconscionable degree. I had always thought you graced with spirit, independence, and intelligence. But Miss Poole has shown me quite out. Your life, Miss Trant, is only what she is making of it."

With a thrust of her arms, she attempted to push him out of her way, unwilling to listen to another word. But he caught her wrists effortlessly and dragged her against him in a crushing embrace. For a moment, she struggled, flailing her arms wildly and thrashing her legs. Then suddenly Nell's eyes met his, which were filled with desire, and she crumpled against him. His hand raised her chin from the folds of his cravat, and she scarcely had time to realize his intent before his lips were stirring against hers.

A shudder shot through her as he kissed her with a consuming hunger that demanded her surrender. She was vaguely surprised that his body shook, that his breath came unsteadily. Then her own need overcame all else, and Nell pressed her fingers into his thick hair while feverishly slipping her tongue over his lips.

"Oh, God, Nell," he moaned thickly, his breath mixing with hers before he drove his lips onto hers again with a brutal, naked longing.

His hands caressed the small of her back, making Nell's

spine tingle with delirious pleasure. Her own hands moved to the nape of his neck and played with the short, rough hairs there. She might even have been so lost as to permit the hand traveling toward her breast to actually rest there had not the abrupt opening of the door startled them both apart.

Her eyes still dilated with passion, her body still throbbing with yearning, Nell stared in blind horror at Miss Poole standing on the threshold. Sir Charles put a hand to her sleeve, but she shook it off with a violent twist. Then, stuffing her fist to her mouth, Nell ran from the room.

# - *11* -

"YOU ARE QUITE certain about this, Miss Trant?"

"Yes," Nell answered without hesitation.

Lord Warwynne did not look the least reassured, but after hesitating another moment, he signaled his tiger to jump down and take the heads of his matched bays. "Very well," he said morosely as he climbed down, then turned to assist Nell from the perch seat of his curricle. "But it ain't quite the thing!"

However, Nell did not waste energy questioning what she was doing. Since yesterday she had known without a doubt that for once Miss Poole was wrong. Sir Charles's marriage to Beth would not purge her own love for him. At first, running from his kiss, his touch, Nell had frantically asked herself what was wrong with her. One moment she longed to see him on the wrong end of a sword point; the other she wished only to feel him in her arms. Self-disgust consumed her.

That he could kiss her so . . . so *ardently* while intending to wed Beth filled her with a physical distress unlike any she had ever known. Her love for him weakened her. She thought she would be unable to endure the pain of this sickening weakness, but a hard core of rage steadied her, giving her a needed focus for her thoughts. It obviously mattered little to him who he held in his arms, and it certainly mattered nothing to her! Or so, through a long and sleepless night, she told herself. In the end, as dawn crept in over her windowsill to become entwined with the flowers on her wallpaper, she admitted that it did matter. Seeing the miserable depths to which her love had sunk her, Nell determined anew that she could not allow Beth to wed the baronet.

Thus it was that she walked beside the disapproving Lord Warwynne in a most unsavory section of London. They paused once more, an imperceptible second, before mounting the set of grimy, chipped steps leading to the unpainted front door of a sadly disreputable building. Before Lord Warwynne could raise any further objections, Nell set her gloved knuckles sharply against the peeling wood. She was rewarded with an almost instant response. The door drew inward by an invisible hand, and she heard his lordship's audible gulp.

With an ungentle hand upon the sleeve of his royal blue broadcloth coat, Nell dragged the viscount into the dimly lit hall. The door swung shut behind them, and they both jumped. A croaked laugh spun them around to face the shortest, most wrinkled gentleman Nell had ever beheld.

"And what, may I make so's bold to ask, are the pair o'ye up to?" demanded the little man.

"I—we—that is to say, she—" Lord Warwynne began.

"We are here to see Mr. Geldsmith. Please inform him that he has callers," Nell said imperiously.

The gentleman yanked a pair of round spectacles from a pocket of his patched brown coat, wiped the lenses ponderously on his sleeve, and settled them upon his large nose. He looked them up, then down, finally bringing his pale eyes to rest on Nell's face.

"Eh! and just who do I say is callin'?" he asked, then laughed as if he had made a grand jest.

"That, sir, is none of your business," she returned with her haughtiest air. "We will deal with Mr. Geldsmith *only*. Now, please, tell him we are here."

"Well, now, mayhap I will, mayhap I won't," came the unperturbed response. He rubbed a gnarled hand over his pointed chin, and suddenly the pale eyes sharpened. "Follow me," he grunted, pushing past them to climb a steep, narrow staircase.

Nell held the skirt of her green-striped walking dress high and tried not to think of the rats that must surely reside in this filth. Her nostrils flared at the foul odors attacking her nose. The wizened old man halted abruptly before a door, drew a brass circle of keys from another of his voluminous pockets, and fit one into the lock. He pressed open the door and stood back to bow them in.

"I say, Miss Tr—I say, I don't think we should—"

"Hush!" Forcibly shoving Warwynne before her, Nell crossed the threshold to the sound of dry laughter behind her.

They stood in a surprisingly clean office which was simply but adequately furnished with three colorfully filled bookcases lining one wall. Before them stood an expansive desk piled with disorderly stacks of papers. With arched brows, Nell sat down in one of the two upholstered chairs placed before the desk and wondered how to greet a moneylender.

As Warwynne sat reluctantly down beside her, a rustling cough brought Nell's head around in time to see the old man discarding the pieced coat of dirty brown, revealing an astonishing long-tailed fuchsia coat trimmed with gold braid.

"Lord! Did Weston make that coat?" his lordship asked, pulling out his quizzing glass to examine the cut more closely. "That's a damned fine job of tailoring!"

"This isn't the time to discuss *coats!*" Nell hissed in exasperation. "Where is Mr. Geldsmith?" she inquired in a louder voice. "I've told you, we will deal with no one else."

The intricate web of wrinkles was etched more deeply into the small, keen face as the old man choked dryly in what Nell faintly realized was laughter. He did not answer, but came across the room to take the high-backed leather chair behind the desk. Finally Nell understood.

"*You!* You are Mr. Geldsmith!" she said, half in disbelief, half in anger at his deception.

"At your service, ma'am, sir," he acknowledged with a little nod to each. His voice had become more refined.

"One can't be too careful, you understand, in these parts of town." He shuffled papers together, moved them around to rest at his elbow, then split his lips in an inquisitive smile. "And just how may I be of service?"

His pale eyes glinted behind the spectacles as they moved from his lordship to Nell. Inhaling courage with a deep breath, she stated flatly, "I should like to borrow twenty thousand pounds."

For a long moment, while Nell's blood deafened her ears and her palms became uncomfortably damp, Geldsmith fiddled with his papers. At length he placed his palms upon the rearranged stack and disconcerted her with a direct stare. "Twenty thousand. Naturally, for so large a sum, I shall require substantial collateral."

She had come prepared for such a request. With a tight lift of her lips, she extracted a bundled document from her reticule. Handing it to Mr. Geldsmith, she said evenly, "That is the deed to my school in Norfolk. There are no debts or mortages standing against it."

With what seemed to Nell the slowest of motions, he undid the thin strip of yellow ribbon and perused the deed. Then, carefully, neatly, he refolded the sheets and retied the ribbon. "This wouldn't be worth a gold-drop to me, miss," he said, shaking his head.

Daunted, but not yet ready to give up, Nell presented Mr. Geldsmith with what she hoped was a captivating smile. "But, sir, I am certain you see that I do not wish to lose my school and will therefore not fail to repay you."

Like fine parchment suddenly embedded in steel, his voice hardened. "I don't believe it pays to deal with angelics. It doesn't pay at all."

"Angelics?" she repeated quickly.

"Unmarried chits," Lord Warwynne explained in an unnecessary stage whisper.

"But I do not see what my married state has to do with this," Nell protested. "I shall repay you, sir, every penny. Including your outrageous interest."

Geldsmith removed his spectacles, withdrew a linen handkerchief from his pocket, and meticulously cleaned them. Resettling them upon his nose, he inspected Nell from the top of her chip bonnet tied with a broad sash of deep green to the tip of her shoe showing beneath the triple flounce of her hem. She had the uncomfortable feeling that he knew to a cent precisely what each item she wore had cost and more over, precisely which dressmaker had made them. Wishing she had worn her best dress, she nonetheless smiled bravely and crossed her fingers in their lime kid gloves.

Suddenly the little man pushed back his chair and stood up. "Without a husband to make good your payment, miss— just in case, you should find yourself unable to pay, you understand—and with nothing more than that useless school for collateral, well, I'm afraid I haven't got your twenty thousand pounds."

Without waiting for a response, he moved quickly to the door, flipping a round gold watch on the end of its fob as he did so. They were clearly dismissed and, though Nell longed to stay and make an impassioned plea, Lord Warwynne was already on his feet, his hand at her elbow. Gritting her teeth, she rose and did not speak again until they were underway in his lordship's fine curricle.

"That—that odious little man!" Nell burst out, unable to contain her disappointment any longer.

"Well, I'm deuced glad he didn't lend it to you. A cent-per-cent's the surest road to ruin. Once they've got their teeth sunk into you, there's no getting free." Glancing at Nell seated mournfully beside him, Warwynne added in quite a different tone, "I daresay I could raise the wind quick enough. I should be honored to do it for you, Miss Trant."

"You are very, very kind. But there is no need for you to bother yourself further on my behalf, my lord."

"I wish you would call me Arthur," the viscount muttered.

They did not speak again until they had stopped before her town house. As his lordship's tiger held the horses still, they sat there a moment longer.

"I must thank you for all your kindness, Arthur," Nell said. "Particularly as I know you were opposed to taking me there."

The viscount colored lightly, then awkwardly took her hand. "You don't think . . . could you possibly reconsider my offer of marriage? M'father would settle a tidy sum upon us, you know."

At that, Nell blushed and bent her head. On sudden

impulse, she brought her free hand up to touch his cheek. "You are so *very* kind. I do wish I could. But . . ."

"But you cannot, eh?" Warwynne said, striving vainly for a cheery note.

"No." Nell sighed. Quickly, she raised her head and placed her lips where her hand had just been. As his lordship went violently red, she loosed her hand from his and climbed nimbly down from the carriage. She ran up the steps without a backward look, certain that if she did so, her tears of frustration would no longer be contained.

Suddenly, to her surprise, Sir Charles stood before her. "May I have a word with you, Miss Trant?" he inquired, his voice oddly unsteady.

Dumbly, she nodded and followed him into the formal sitting room. She stood, uncertain, in the center of the faded carpet, twisting the silk cord of her reticule in her hands and watching warily as the baronet wandered to the window. His hand played aimlessly with the edge of the pulled drape, but though the action was casual, his stance was not. The seams of his chestnut morning coat seemed stretched to their utmost limit over his set shoulders, and the tensed muscles encased in fawn pantaloons seemed almost ready to snap. Twisting her hands together, Nell opened her mouth to ask what he wanted when he spoke without turning.

"I was standing here but ten minutes ago."

At first she did not understand, but slowly she realized he had had a full view of her return with Lord Warwynne. Wondering wildly what construction he had put on what he must have seen, she could think of nothing to say. "Oh," was all she managed at the end of a monstrous pause.

He pivoted and faced her then. His heavy lids hid the expression in his eyes, and his features were immobile, unreadable. "I presume I am to wish you happy," he said without inflection.

Astounded, Nell could only stare at him in speechless surprise. She had been thinking how to lead him away from the truth of her expedition to the moneylender, but she had not thought of anything as incredible as *this!* Hot spots of color stained her cheeks. His went pale.

"I see I am," he said flatly. He came toward her while she floundered to correct his mistake, but he robbed her of the breath to speak as he continued, "I do wish you happy,

Nell. It has not always seemed so in the past, I know, but I have ever wished you well. I only ask you to..." His voice faded as he went white about the mouth.

"To what?" whispered Nell.

"To be certain," he finished sharply. "Warwynne is a green coxcomb and—"

"Lord Warwynne is quite the kindest man of my acquaintance," Nell interrupted in instant defense.

His face went tight, but with a visible grip on his control, he said with quiet calm, "Yes. I'm sorry. I do not wish to quarrel with you again, Nell. I proffer you my... my sincere wishes for your future happiness."

Two strides had him at the door before Nell cried out, "Wait!"

He halted, but did not look at her. She drew in a deep breath.

"You—you are laboring under a misconception, Charles."

He spun round at that, his face deathly pale against his black cravat, his vivid blue eyes piercing her with a question.

"I am not marrying Warwynne." Not a muscle in him moved, so she struggled on. "He—he did honor me with an offer, but I—I couldn't accept. Beyond the fact that he is so young, beyond that, well, I do not—not have the regard for him that a wife should hold for a husband."

Though, while speaking, she had looked nervously at everything but the baronet, she fixed a steady eye on him at this last. He did not flinch, as she thought he would, considering his own loveless match, but he completely disconcerted her by coming swiftly to stand directly before her. With a gentle hand, he untied the bow of her chip bonnet and drew the hat from her head.

"I apologize for my premature congratulations. I shall know next time to wait until I read the notice in the *Gazette.*"

His off-center smile knocked all her senses off balance. Once again he was relaxed and in control, and she wondered at the oddity of him. He set her bonnet on the cushion of the settee, then collected one of her hands and began slowly to draw off her glove.

She pulled her trembling hand free from his warm grasp and twirled to sit down next to her hat. She dropped her reticule upon the settee and looked at nothing in particular. Hoping he could not see how her pulses were throbbing, she attempted a coquettish giggle. "Really, Sir Charles, you are most perplexing."

He laughed in reply, then strolled over to lean against the mantel of the fireplace. Eyeing her as she removed her gloves and lay them neatly on the brim of her hat, he remarked lazily, "So you do not love the puppy. And did not, I take it, feel you could come to care for him?"

Confused by his gentle tone, his softened glance in her direction, Nell answered before she realized what she was saying. "I cannot give what has already been taken by another."

Her palm flew to cover her mouth as if to hold back any more incriminating words. Staring at him over her hand, she saw that all the rigidity had returned to his figure. His face was a replica of the bronze statue of a Roman soldier Papa had had in his library before selling it to pay for a night at Boodle's.

"Another? Are you saying you love someone else?" Sir Charles demanded.

"I—I . . ." she faltered.

In one long step he had reached her, taken her hands, and yanked her to her feet. "Who is he?" he rasped.

Jerking her hands from his searing touch, Nell scowled at him. "Really! This is none of your business! You've no right to press me on such a matter!"

A series of expressions flashed over his face—frustration, anger, longing, and finally a hint of optimism. "Come, Nellie, I'm only seeking to help you if I can. As a friend." His voice caressed her even as his hand possessed hers.

Striving to find an answer that would satisfy him, yet not reveal her hopeless love for him, Nell was disturbed by the tender stroking of his thumb over the center of her palm. Even her ready temper failed to rescue her, for she could not maintain an animosity she did not truly feel when he was being so unbearably irresistible. Her distress was plain. Seeing it, Sir Charles bent closer to her until she felt the warmth of his breath on her earlobe, smelled the starched cleanliness of his cravat.

"Tell me," he coaxed in a loving murmur. "Tell me who has won your heart."

Her knees turned to water and she felt herself weaken. But, said a voice that would not be silenced within her, think how he will laugh when he learns of your undying love! Nell stiffened.

"I cannot," she mumbled into his too-near shoulder.

"But of course you can, my sweet friend."

This time his lips grazed her earlobe, and an uncontrollable shiver coursed through her. Knowing how determined he could be, she forced herself to step back, look into his eyes, and state firmly, "I cannot, Sir Charles, for if truth must be told, the gentleman in question does not return my regard." She looked away. That, at least, was true enough. "He—he would have someone else." Still true. Almost anyone else. She faced him again. "I do not wish to humiliate myself by exposing my—my unreturned affections."

What did she see flare in his eyes, turning them to bits of blue fire? She could not determine if it was hope or resentment at not having his way. The baronet swept a hand over his eyes, hiding their secrets from her, then slowly lowered it to gaze intently at her.

"Let's have done with these games, Nell," he said in a weary voice. "I cannot bear this hellish charade any longer."

"Games?" she echoed, not understanding his new mood.

Gentleness fell from him; he captured her arm in a fierce grip before she could step away. "Yes, by God!"

Confusion became mingled with fright in her eyes, but she lifted her chin, swallowed around the lump in her throat, and requested her instant release. In reply, the hand circling her arm tightened its hold, and Sir Charles gave her a little shake that rattled her teeth. But Nell freed herself with a mighty wrench of her arm and snatched up her bonnet, bag and gloves, preparing to leave at once.

"You say you do not wish to quarrel with me, sir, but that is all you ever do," she said with a breathless sob. "But I am not in the mood for arguing. Pray find someone else on whom to vent your ill humor!"

She took two quick steps, expecting him to stop her. When he did not, she halted, whirled round, and demanded with something very like despair, "*Why* must you confuse me so? One moment you are cruel, the next you are kind. I never know what it is you want from me."

"Forgive me, Nell," he returned in a tone of soft intimacy.

Ignoring him, she strode restlessly around the room. "How can you kiss me when you are to marry Beth? How can you marry at all when you do not *care?* Do you understand the meaning of marriage, Sir Charles? I don't think you even understand the meaning of friendship! Though you claim to be my friend, all you do is argue with me!"

She stopped and fixed a reproving eye upon him. Let him explain himself if he could! But her breath caught in her throat as she grasped the full measure of his gaze. Like an unclouded summer sky, his eyes shone a clear blue, brilliant with promise.

"If you were not such a firebrand, dearest Nell, we should not argue so often," he responded with a chuckle that seemed to reach out and touch her.

"If *that* is your idea of either an apology or an explanation, then I am surely wasting my time here," she retorted with a huff. Hat and gloves clutched tightly in one hand, reticule clenched in the other, she once again reached the door. "Good day, Sir Charles."

This time he did stop her. "Stay a moment!" he bid in warm command. As she turned very slowly to face him, he went on, his voice low and melting. "I desire nothing less than to have further quarrels with you, Nell. Surely, you must see that I want something far different for us. You must realize that—"

At that instant, the door swept open, meeting painfully with Nell's shoulder.

"Eleanor! I did not hurt you, did I?" Miss Poole inquired anxiously as she peered round the door's edge.

"No, no. It was a mere bump, that is all," she replied in a distracted voice.

"Are you certain, dearest?" put in Beth, following on Miss Poole's heels. "It would be dreadful to take a bruise and spoil the effect of your ball gown."

"Yes! Don't fuss so!" snapped her sister in vexation. She longed to throw them bodily from the room and discover what Sir Charles had been about to say. The ardent tone of his voice, the dark glow of his eyes, even the vibrancy of his stance, had all given a heavy significance to his words, and now she would never know what he had been about to say. Already, he had resumed his casual air of boredom, greeting Beth with a light kiss on her hand.

"You need not raise your voice to Miss Elizabeth," reproached Drusilla with a frown. Her eyes darted meaningfully from Nell to Sir Charles, unknowingly increasing Nell's irritation with her.

Incapable of maintaining social conversation after her double disappointments, Nell quickly excused herself, assuring them all again that her shoulder was unhurt. She sought the solitude of her own chambers, feeling more muddled than ever. She had been nearly undone by Sir Charles's gentle tenderness. For a moment she had come much too close to blurting out her love to him, which she must never do. How he would laugh! How it would amuse him to learn that, after jilting him, she now ached to be in his arms.

## - 12 -

As was always the case, the exclusive temple of the *beau monde* shone with company wonderfully select. Here one's rank and wealth did not automatically procure entrance, for only acceptance by its patronesses could guarantee admittance into the sacrosanct Almack's. Eleanor Trant, however, was not feeling properly struck with gratitude to be among the chosen. Since coming to London it seemed she had been constantly in either a state of high dudgeon or a fit of the dismals. Tonight, seated with a glass of lemonade in one hand and her fan in the other, she watched the colorful whirl and twirl of dance after dance and suffered the doldrums. Her failure to gain the necessary funds from the odious Mr. Geldsmith weighed heavily upon her spirits.

One brief moment of cheer had lifted her when, in the act of stifling a heavy sigh, she caught sight of Mr. Perkins entering the assembly rooms, in attendance upon Lady Harlowe. Nell had pressed her mother, seated beside her, into signaling to the rotund baroness and, as the newcomers came toward them, the Trant ladies set aside their glasses of lemonade and rose. Since the last occasion of their meeting had been the night at Drury Lane, the gentleman eyed Nell warily as she presented him with the first real smile she had worn that day. Still cherishing hopes of matching him with Beth, Nell captured his black velvet sleeve with one gloved hand and summoned up a coy laugh.

"What a pleasant surprise to be sure, Mr. Perkins. We have seen too little of you these past weeks." She nudged her sister with an elbow and prompted, "Haven't we missed seeing Mr. Perkins, Beth, dear?"

The cornette of lace and pleated rose ribbon scarcely moved as Elizabeth acknowledged Mr. Perkins with a tiny, stiff bend of her head. This was not at all promising, and Nell tried to cover her sister's lack of warmth with a suffusion of her own. "But of course you will dance with us tonight! We shall take it very amiss should you forget us." She ended with a deliberately coy giggle then tapped his knuckles with her fan.

"I should, of course, be sorry to disappoint you," said Mr. Perkins in the tones of a man who has been granted a stay of execution, "but I am here to attend Lady Harlowe and must give my attention to my duty."

"Nonsense, dear boy!" interposed that pleasant-faced lady with a swish of tulle shawl over purple satin gown. "You think too much of work. Now that we are here, I insist that you enjoy yourself."

"But my lady—"

"You are not to fret over me, Mr. Perkins. I shall do very well indeed, for Mrs. Trant and I have just agreed to repair to the card room for a hand of piquet." With a lightness of foot surprising for one of her figure, Lady Harlowe departed, with Eugenia Trant strolling languidly behind.

Nell seized her opportunity without a second's hesitation. "There, you shall dance with us after all, Mr. Perkins. Nothing could be more perfect. Now, I insist that you lead out Beth—yes, dearest I *insist,*" she said firmly as Beth raised a trembling hand in protest. "I shall have my dance with Mr. Perkins later."

As she spoke Nell thrust the two together then resumed her seat and followed their progress. She reflected that Mr. Perkins must surely be unable to resist Beth tonight, for she looked quite stunning in a white crepe gown festooned with wreaths of roses along the hem. If only he had *money*, Nell thought with frustration. She absently collected her glass of lemonade and permitted herself to give vent to a repressed sigh.

The crowd stirred, a rustle of whispering voices rose, and all heads moved in one direction. Nell paused in the act of listlessly taking a sip of her drink and followed the general motion, turning to see a woman poised at the entrance as if caught and held still for one breathtaking instant. From the silver comb adorning the midnight curls vividly streaked with gray, to the deep blue sheath with the spangled gauze overdress ornamenting the delicately petite figure, she was superbly lovely. As she stood as still as a statue, the new cynosure of Almack's leisurely surveyed the rooms with a pair of dazzling blue eyes. Seconds later, she was at Nell's side.

"Dear Miss Trant, how glad I am you have come! It's been an age, child." Lady Sarah Grayson's laughter sounded like chimes in the wind and never failed to captivate. Nell's glass was plucked from her hand, given imperiously to the baronet standing beside his mother, and Nell was pulled without ceremony to her feet. "How lovely you are looking! You should not be hiding all this beauty in that outlandish school."

Despite her downcast mood, Nell answered the laugh with one of her own. "But never, Lady Grayson, as lovely as you. You remain the most ravishing woman in London, you know."

The sapphire eyes shimmered with self-amusement. "Now, how am I to respond to that, my dear? If I agree, then I am truly puffed up in my own conceit; but if I disagree, I am overly modest. But I don't wish to speak of me at all. Where did you get this amazingly stunning dress? Do turn around for me."

With some reluctance, for the enchanting Lady Grayson had already drawn a circle of admirers about her, Nell obeyed her command. As she rotated, she felt all their stares upon her, palpably sizing, judging, and she was grateful that her mother had refused to let her wear her India muslin one more time. Declaring that it would be a disgrace to the Trant name should Eleanor be seen in that dress yet again, Mama had ordered Madame Despois to create something suitable whether the silly child wished for it or no. Madame Despois had proven herself more than equal to the task.

The very height of fashion, the gown was round, with short, slashed sleeves and a deeply cut neck that draped low over the shoulders and back. The deep green iridescent satin, which glistened and glimmered with Nell's slightest motion, made it unique and particularly flattering to her. Its radiance reflected the crystal glow of her green eyes while enhancing the burnished copper of her coiled hair. When she ceased to spin round, Nell found herself facing the appreciative gaze of Sir Charles. Momentarily disconcerted, she dropped her lashes and, though she refused to look up again, she remained vividly aware of his smallest gesture.

She wondered how any gentleman could appear so supremely handsome in black satin breeches and king's-blue velvet, then immediately took herself to task for caring a rap how he looked. But from the pearl buttons studding the front of his cream silk waistcoat to the clocks worked elaborately into the white silk of his stockings, she knew him to be the most handsome man in the room, and not the severest self-scold could stop her from acknowledging it in her heart.

"Stunning, Miss Trant, truly stunning!" declared Lady Grayson with another tinkling laugh. She took Nell's hand and led her back to a row of seats lining the wall. "Now we must have a comfortable coze before I release you to all the beaux who are no doubt wishing me to perdition. Tell me all about your school, my child, and whether you are happy."

Both her tone and look were unexpectedly serious, but Nell sat beside Lady Grayson and did her best to relate three years' worth of experiences in as many minutes. While speaking, she caught a glimpse of Beth dancing with Mr. Perkins and smiled. But her smile vanished as her eyes fell upon Sir Charles chatting amiably with Miss Martha Norton, a young miss whose blond locks struck Nell as sadly insipid and whose character was obviously outrageously *fast*. Suddenly she realized she had fallen silent and returned her attention to Lady Grayson, a pink flush slowly covering her features.

"I'm sorry. Did you ask me something?"

"As a matter of fact, I did, child," admitted Lady Grayson, who was watching her closely, "but you were busily looking at that scamp of a son of mine and did not hear."

Nell dropped her eyes to her lap and knew a burning

shame. To be caught staring at him! She was filled with self-revulsion, but Lady Grayson passed over her humiliation as if it were nothing, repeating her query casually.

"I asked if everything was in order for Friday night, my dear. Is there anything I might do to aid you in the last minute preparations?"

"Thank you, but I believe there is little left to do. You need only arrive at the ball and enjoy yourself," Nell replied as she strove to regain her composure. "Mama, of course, is quite worn out with merely thinking about it."

"And how is your mother? Is she at home?"

"No. She is in the card room, playing for pennies with the same enthusiasm she plays for pounds. Card playing is the one activity in which Mama exerts herself."

"Then I must go in and see her," Lady Grayson announced, rising as she spoke. Her hand fluttered and, as if in response to some signal, Sir Charles appeared. "Ah, there you are, Charles. I think perhaps it is time Miss Trant enjoyed herself. I've monopolized her to a shocking degree when I'm certain she would far rather have been dancing."

"Oh, no, Lady Grayson," Nell began in protest, but the words fell into empty air. Her ladyship had sailed off, leaving Nell staring up at the one man she most wished to avoid.

She had not seen him since yesterday's confrontation in the sitting room and was uncertain how to respond to the warmth in his eyes. Her own mood was somewhat less than cordial, for she very much resented his ability to reduce her heartbeat to a mere echo with only a look. Moreover, she knew that if she succeeded in putting a stop to his betrothment before the ball on Friday, she would be leaving for Norfolk within the week. And though she told herself that should be cause for rejoicing, she simply felt more dispirited than ever.

"Would you care to dance, Miss Trant?" he asked with a formal bow contradicted by the twinkle in his azure eyes.

"I—er, I—," she sputtered, twisting her hands over the sticks of her fan.

"Indecisive, Miss Trant?" he murmured as he put out his hand. "How very unlike you, my dear."

She did not take the proffered hand, but wound her fingers more tightly around her fan. "Of course not!" she said peevishly, looking about the rooms as if seeking an avenue of escape. "It's just that—just that I've already promised this dance to someone else."

"Oh, and may I ask to whom? Your partner seems lamentably late in coming to claim his dance," Sir Charles said with the suggestion of a laugh. Nell's head snapped up, but her anger, her will to resist, faded before the intensity of his dark gaze.

Rescue materialized in the form of Mr. Perkins, with Beth on his arm. Although she saw the unusual color mantling her sister's woeful face, Nell did not take the time to consider the cause. She stood up and forced a laugh. "But here is my partner now, Sir Charles. I had begun to think, Mr. Perkins, you were going to forget my dance."

She took his arm and whisked him away before he could utter a disclaimer. As they moved toward the set forming, however, Nell noted that her escort held himself even more stiffly than usual. Casting a swift glance at his profile, she saw a swarthy stain upon his skin. As he looked down at her, the cleft in his chin seemed more deeply graven. She paused, then stopped altogether.

"Would you rather sit out this dance, Mr. Perkins?" she asked in a quiet voice. "I do not truly wish to dance, you know."

He appeared not to care, responding to her inquiry with a monosyllable that could well have passed for a grunt. They retired, instead, to a sofa, where they settled in silence. Across the room, Nell saw her sister sitting beside Sir Charles. She still looked unaccountably ablush, far more so than could have been attributed to the exertion of the country dance. Keeping her eyes fixed on her sister, Nell remarked calmly, "Beth does not look herself this evening, Mr. Perkins. I do wonder if she is feeling out of sorts."

"I would not know," he responded shortly.

"Would you not?" Nell faced him. "But I think perhaps you would. She did not look so cast down before your dance."

Though she would not have thought it possible, the gentleman sat more rigidly than before. When he did not comment, Nell swept her eyes over the ever-changing kaleidoscope of dancers and said evenly, "If, perhaps, my sister has behaved with impropriety—"

His head jerked around and he cut in with suppressed rage, "Miss Elizabeth has made known her opinion that it is *I* who have acted indecorously!"

"Oh!" said Nell, taken aback. After a moment she ventured cautiously, "May I inquire as to the nature of her . . . her exact comments?"

He emitted a short, bitter laugh. "I make no doubt she will shortly favor you—perhaps everyone!—with her views, ma'am. She believes that I have allowed—no, *encouraged* attentions from yourself, Miss Trant. It is her opinion that I am little better than a blackguard out to break your heart."

"Did—did she actually say *that?*"

"Not in so many words," he admitted through clenched teeth. "But her meaning was clear enough, ma'am. Vividly clear!"

Nell paled. This was a complication she had never envisioned. That Beth should be jealous of *her!* She leaned toward Mr. Perkins and gently laid her hand upon his tense arm. "Perhaps if I were to speak with her, explain to her that you have never given me the least cause—"

"Oh, there is no need to put yourself out, ma'am. It does not matter to me what she thinks. If she chooses to believe me such a pretty sort of fellow, it is all one with me."

His tightened jaw and his furious gaze belied this impassioned declaration. But Nell had no chance to point this out to the gentleman, for it seemed that, once loosened, his intemperate tongue had no wish to stop.

"As if *she* has any room to criticize others! She cares only for wealth and luxury. True love means less than nothing to her. No, she chooses a man whose reputation casts the worst indiscretion of mine in the shade."

Suddenly it occurred to Nell that she had never heard Mr. Perkins speak so fervently, with such little care for the propriety of his words. It dawned on her that jealousy and wounded pride had acted powerfully upon him, and she turned a thoughtful eye upon her sister across the way. Just then both Beth and Sir Charles happened to look in her direction. Nell seized upon the moment. She pressed more closely to Mr. Perkins, gazed soulfully up into his wrathful face, and begged him to becalm himself. Artfully unfurling her fan, she hid their expressions from view and said quite briskly that if he wished to make so great a cake of himself, it was all very well and good, but she would have thought he would have done better to show Miss Beth a thing or two.

"What do you mean?" he demanded. The angry glint in his hazel eyes sharpened to a suspicious curiosity.

"Why, only that if Beth thinks you such a womanizer, then you should act the part! She would soon realize that you are not the man to be so insulted."

Swallowing her impatience, Nell held her breath while he considered her words. He was obviously torn between the dread of behaving improperly and the desire to show Elizabeth Trant how little her words could wound him. He was still visibly wavering when a shadow fell over them.

"I trust you enjoyed your dance," said Sir Charles dryly.

Nell's fan descended slowly, revealing a pair of flushed faces. Her lips curved slightly and she said airily, "Oh, we enjoyed ourselves vastly, I assure you."

A sharp hiss of breath brought Nell's eyes round to meet Beth's accusing stare. Her cornflower-blue eyes were darkened by a disbelieving hurt, and at last Nell felt as if she were making progress. Telling herself it was for Beth's good, she forced a bright smile to her lips. "We had no wish to step out in a Scots reel when we might be more together here, did we, Josiah?"

She faced him with a smile still plastered to her mouth, but with her hard eyes commanding him to fall in with her plans. Her body felt limp with relief when, after an infinitesimal hesitation, he said, "No, we did not...Eleanor." Valiantly he infused his voice with a vestige of warmth.

"How touching," the baronet commented in tones of iron. "But I believe this is my dance, Miss Trant—unless you wish to sit this one out with *me*."

"I do not think she wishes to do either," put in Mr. Perkins with rare belligerency.

Taking in the sudden blanching of her sister's previously crimson cheeks, Nell quickly disagreed. "Oh, but I would welcome a dance. I do feel the need of some exercise."

Jumping to her feet, she put out a hand to Sir Charles, while Mr. Perkins committed himself wholeheartedly to his part by rising beside her, glowering at the baronet and saying truculently, "I shall await your return to my side."

"Oh, la, Josiah, you say the most precious things," trilled Nell. Catching the shock upon Beth's face, Nell became instantly certain she had missed her true vocation. Should the school fail, she would turn to the stage.

Abruptly, her hand was clamped to the baronet's side, and she was hauled firmly away. Before she could remonstrate, he swept away her very breath by stating harshly, "I applaud you on your admirable performance, Miss Trant, and can only wonder that you waste yourself on so small an audience."

With remarkable restraint, she contented herself with a mere glare at the baronet's handsome profile as he led her into the quadrille. Since Lady Jersey had introduced this French dance at Almack's the year before, it had become one of the most popular and was considered a must at every dancing class. Miss Trant, however, needed no lessons, for she executed the steps with her usual light grace which, considering the turbulent state of her emotions, was no insignificant feat.

Uncertain whether to give herself up to the joy of simply being near Sir Charles or the sorrow of counting the moments of what in all likelihood must be their last dance together, Nell's feelings changed from laughter to tears with each turn of the dance. And all the while Sir Charles's taunting comment plagued her, making her dizzy with worry.

If he suspected her regard for Mr. Perkins was a sham, it would ruin everything. Somehow she must convince him—and Beth—otherwise. Tonight and tomorrow were all she had left in which to bring her sister to her senses. After several wordless turns, she finally addressed her partner.

"You think, then, that I overplayed my hand." A thread of a sigh escaped her.

His brows shot upward; his lids drew downward. "You never ceased to amaze me, my dear. No other lady of my acquaintance would have admitted her deception."

"But, you see, I do so for selfish reasons. I wish to ask your advice."

From beneath the fringe of her lowered lashes, she saw to her satisfaction that she had truly amazed him. A quizzical caution stole over his features as he inquired tonelessly,

"Indeed? And how may I be of service?"

"You may recall that I spoke to you of . . . of my affection for a certain gentleman," she explained breathlessly. His face went taut, his mouth became set in an uncompromising line, and she went on in a rush before courage failed her altogether. "I told you then that he did not care for me in return. Well, tonight he has at last . . . favored me with a show of regard, and I fear I may have put him off by being . . . too *forward*. But I was uncertain, you see, how best to encourage him."

The last words sounded a little desperate even to her own ears, for as she spoke, the baronet's grip upon her hand tightened until she felt certain she had been bruised. Her speech rang with compelling distress, and Sir Charles reacted as if he had been slapped. He dropped her hand without ceremony and turned his back on her, leaving her standing in midstep. She raced after him, catching his arm and trying vainly to act as if nothing untoward were occurring.

"What on earth are you *doing?* Do you want to cause a scene *here,* of all places!" she hissed in his ear, then grinned foolishly at Mrs. Drummond Burrell in passing, hoping the *grande dame* saw nothing amiss. "Well? Answer me!"

He stopped with such abruptness that Nell was thrown slightly off balance as she skidded to a halt beside him. With cold precision, he ran his eyes from the top of her neatly coiled hair to the bottom of her vandyked hem, then back again to rest on her face. His eyes were the blue of a darkly frozen river, and Nell saw nothing but a disgust of her within them.

"You have no need to ask advice on how to encourage a man, my little sweet," he ground out in a furious whisper. "You have been doing so with rare abandonment since you came out of the schoolroom."

"How dare you—you of all people!—censure my behavior!" Nell returned in an equally irate undertone.

"If you truly want my advice, Miss Trant—"

"I don't!"

"—then I suggest you put that poor fool out of his misery before he believes you to be sincere."

"I am sincere, sir!"

"You, my love, have never been sincere," countered the

white-lipped baronet. He detached her hand from his sleeve as if it repulsed him and paused to throw over his shoulder, "You don't know the meaning of the word, Nell."

Then he was gone, leaving her standing alone in the midst of the colorful swirl of dancers.

# - 13 -

SOMEHOW, DESPITE FEELING deprived of the power to move or speak, Nell managed to return with carefully measured steps to the sofa where Mr. Perkins awaited her. She saw no sign of Beth and tried to pretend she neither saw nor heard the covert glances and furtive whispers of the people around her. All the while her hurt and humiliation festered like an uncleaned wound. Calmly accepting Mr. Perkins's offer to dance, placidly nodding to this acquaintance or that, Nell burned with a longing to flay all the malicious gossipmongers. But her fury with Sir Charles blazed even higher.

How dare he walk away from her in the middle of a dance! How could he be so lost to all propriety as to leave her stranded at the center of the *ton's* most prattling clique?

Not once did Nell give any indication that she was mentally skewering Sir Charles Grayson on the end of a pointed spear. With her head high, she danced and chattered with so much animation that what could have easily become a scandalous incident died stillborn.

It was well after midnight before Nell remembered her sister. When she did, remorse engulfed her. How could she be so enmeshed in the tangled web of her own problems as to forget Beth? Her hands clenched into white-knuckled fists, and her face colored with shame as she recognized the depths of her own selfishness. As she was at that moment once again at Mr. Perkins's side, she begged him to excuse her. He did not do so, however, but regarded her with a slight frown.

"What is it, Miss Trant?" he finally inquired kindly. "Do you feel unwell?"

"No, no. It's just that I need to find Elizabeth." His face became set in a hard mask. "Have you seen her?"

"No."

She turned her eyes upon the crowd, scanning the belles and beaux whisking through the room in a country dance, then searching the crush of lookers-on. Nowhere was the young miss to be seen, which increased Nell's anxiety and guilt. "Where can she have got to?" she whispered, wanting only to find her and retreat from this nightmare.

Then it occurred to her that Sir Charles, too, was not to be found amongst those in the assembly rooms, and, despite her best intentions, a spurt of jealousy shot through her. Stiff with new purpose, she faced Mr. Perkins.

"Sir, you were right. I do feel unwell and must retire. Would you excuse me? I shall go now to my mother, then home."

"But of course," he answered, his voice expressionless. "Permit me to take you to your mother."

They had crossed but halfway to the card room when they came upon Mrs. Trant making desultory progress toward them.

"So there you are at last," she sighed heavily.

"I was coming to ask you if we might go home," Nell said quickly. "I feel unwell and . . . I think perhaps Beth has already gone on."

"Why, yes," returned her mother, looking surprised. Then her heavy lids drooped over the curiously alert eyes and she added in fatigued tones, "She, too, felt unwell. Isn't it odd? I trust you are not both catching something. But Sir Charles saw Elizabeth home quite some time ago. Did you not know?"

Nell avoided her mother's sharp gaze by turning to bid Mr. Perkins goodnight. He continued on into the card room to find Lady Harlowe while the Trant ladies departed for home. The carriage ride was unusually silent, with Nell only once coming out of her private reverie to inquire how much her mother had lost at piquet.

"My dear child, such presumption! I do not always lose," her mother responded in something of a huff.

"You would not have left a winning hand, Mama," Nell pointed out with only half-interest. "But since Almack's does not allow anything beyond penny stakes, you can't have gone aground."

She relapsed into meditative silence, while on the opposite seat, Mama appeared to have fallen asleep. But as they were nearing Mount Street, she suddenly pierced Nell with one of her amazingly awake stares and announced, "Sir Charles made it known to me this evening that he wishes for the wedding to take place as soon as possible."

Nell felt as if someone had punched the air from her abdomen. She gasped for breath, for sense, and was grateful for the nightshadows hiding her expression.

"Did—did he say how soon?" she managed in a voice barely more than a croak.

"He put forth his desire to be wed within the month."

"And—and Beth? Did she express her desires?"

"No," confessed her mother with a yawn. "But she was feeling poorly, dear thing, and it is not to be wondered at if she could not speak a word. Still, I am certain she does not object. Elizabeth is such a sweet child, never objecting to anything. So unlike you, Eleanor, so very unlike you."

For once, Nell did not rise to this unfair rebuke. Her mind was spinning, her earlier sense of desperation reinforced. She had always known that, once engaged, Beth would never break her commitment to Sir Charles. But this! Mama, of course, was right. Beth would not object to whatever date was chosen for her wedding. Now, in truth, Nell felt ill.

When at last the coach rolled to a stop, she alighted and followed her mother into the house without being conscious of the steps she took. A thick fog of depression had settled over her, muffling her senses as she mounted the stairs. She did not at first perceive Drusilla Poole awaiting her by the door of her bedchamber. After she had been addressed twice she finally recognized her friend.

"You should not have stayed up, Drusilla. There was no need," she said listlessly.

"It was not a matter of need, Eleanor, but of desire. I wished to speak with you."

Though it was the last thing she wanted at this moment, Nell beckoned her friend into her room, then requested Dru to speak out while she removed her gloves and began to undo the intricate coils of her hair.

"I wanted to tell you that I have decided to return to Norfolk once the matter of the ball is over. I have, in fact, booked a place on the Royal Mail for Saturday morning."

Nell felt Drusilla's eyes following her about the room as she discarded her ball clothes and donned her shapeless white mull nightdress. She knew what her friend wanted, but an unreasonable stubbornness took hold of her, and she refused to say it. At last Drusilla put it into words.

"I should like, Eleanor, for you to accompany me."

Nell gazed into the mirror above her vanity and studied Drusilla's reflection. Concerned, capable, conscientious, and critical—these traits were reflected in the erect bearing, the neat appearance, the compressed lips. Nell had always known that Drusilla, though truly fond of her, disapproved of her temper and her vivacity. Yet their friendship had held together through the years since they were schoolgirls. She found herself wondering why, even as she recognized with a sense of shock that she did not want to return to her life in Norfolk. She had neither the patience nor the temperament to run a school; but more, she simply did not *want* to do it.

These thoughts overwhelmed her. She longed to cry out, "No, I shan't be going back to Norfolk!" Instead she gazed into the mirrored eyes of Miss Poole and said hoarsely, "Yes. Book a place for me. We shall leave Saturday."

A flash of triumph ignited Drusilla's pale eyes, and Nell dropped her own to the scratched top of the vanity. Slowly, her hand clasped a hairbrush, and she began to stroke her copper curls. She did not turn or raise her head when the door opened and then clicked shut.

When she had counted one hundred long, leisurely strokes upon her unruly hair, she set down the brush and rose. She cast a glance at her bed, then one at the door. Hesitating a heartbeat longer, Nell suddenly shivered, then strode to the door.

From the darkened threshold of Beth's room it appeared that she was fast asleep. Indeed, she was curled up beneath her coverlet, her round cheek resting on one hand, much as it had when she was a child. But when Nell's eyes adjusted to the darkness, she caught the rapid movement of the covers and knew her sister was no more able to sleep than she. She crossed the shadows with measured steps, as if giving each footfall great consideration.

As she neared the bedside, she thought she detected a stirring, but it was quickly stifled. Finally, just a breath away from Beth's side, she said softly, "Dearest, I know you are awake. Mama said you did not feel well and I've come to ask if I might be of help."

The stretch of silence that followed seemed darker than the night. Nell did not move; she scarcely breathed. Then, at last, a whisper floated up to her. "No, thank you."

"May I stay a moment, Beth? Do you feel up to conversing with me?" As she spoke, Nell perched on the edge beside her sister, and she felt a rustling motion as Beth twisted to sit upright.

"If you must," she said.

"Shall we have a light, or would you prefer the darkness?" Nell thought she saw a hand quiver. Taking this for assent, she rose and groped among the objects lying atop a small bedside stand until she found the desired flint and candle. As she lit the wick, she faced the bed so that, as the candle flame flicked the black shadows away, she could watch her sister's face. She read both sadness and apprehension in Beth's clouded eyes and downturned lips, and she felt hope wake within her.

Reclaiming her seat on the edge of the bed, she confided, "I actually wanted to discuss something of importance to me, something that I feel cannot wait. I have been thinking for some time that I was not truly suited to running a school. Oh, I know you will think me suffering some odd fancy, but it isn't that at all. I have not the patience, the aptitude for such a life. And it is because I feel unsuited to continue on with my school that I want"—she ended with a large expulsion of breath—"to ask your advice regarding Mr. Perkins."

Beth's sadness became pronounced. Her face took on a sepulchral cast as she nodded wordlessly.

"I have been thinking, dearest, of how *good* a gentleman he is and what a *worthy* husband he would make."

"You have?" Beth asked funereally.

"Yes," Nell replied with an emphatic nod. "And I have quite decided that I should marry him."

"You have?" Beth repeated, this time in a shocked voice.

"Yes, and it is upon this matter that I wished to ask your advice. You see, I know how deeply you respect him—"

"I do not possibly see what advice I could give you," Elizabeth objected with some force. Her voice shook, her eyes fastened on the hand pleating her flowered chintz coverlet.

"Well, of course, Mr. Perkins has not yet asked me, or even given me the slightest encouragement. But he has confided that he no longer has any attachments..." Her voice faded and Beth flinched. Gratified, Nell pressed on. "I am given to hope that, when he sees how much he has come to mean to me, he will be willing to settle for a ... well, a comfortable match."

A heavy pall seemed to settle over the two sisters. Each silent moment seemed magnified by the intensity of emotion between them. At length Elizabeth raised her eyes, dimmed to a dreary shade by her unspoken sorrow. Her lips quivered. "Do you love him?" she asked tremulously. "Do you think he might love you?"

"But I do not look for his love, my dear. Indeed, Mr. Perkins could not give it, for he is just the sort of man who only loves *once*, if you understand my meaning. And, of course, he has already done so..." Again, Nell let her words drift between them as she watched Beth covertly. Satisfied with the mournful pallor she saw stealing over her young sister's face, she continued in brisk tones, "But I am hopeful that he could come to be fond of me, and I am certain we could deal tolerably well together."

"D-deal well t-together?"

"Yes, as husband and wife."

Once again a shroud of silence fell between them. Taking note of her sister's distressed appearance, Nell felt better and better. Hope rang cheerily through her next words.

"But Mr. Perkins is like all men. You may depend upon it that *he* shall never think of offering for me! And that is why I've come to you, dearest. If you could give him the merest hint, a suggestion that his suit should not be unwelcome to me..."

This time Nell did not wait for her sister to respond. She

pressed a kiss against Beth's unnaturally cold cheek and stood up. Blowing out the wavering light with a brisk puff, she hoped that this time she might succeed. She could not doubt the depth of Beth's love. Her sorrowing heart had revealed itself. If this did not spur Beth into crying off from her match with Sir Charles, there was nothing left for Nell to do but accept the dictates of a malicious Fate. But as she returned to her own room, she felt better than she had in days.

Her optimism did not last. Though Beth appeared for breakfast the next morning looking sadly wan, with half-circles ringing her eyes, she drained Nell of hope by informing her that she was sending a note round for Mr. Perkins, asking him to call.

"Oh, you are going to speak for me," Nell said in hollow tones.

"Yes," said Beth, failing to meet her sister's eye.

Nell lost the opportunity to scotch this plan when Miss Poole and her father entered. Wearing an unusual smile upon her wide mouth, Drusilla began speaking long before she reached her seat at the table.

"My congratulations to you, Elizabeth," she said. "Your dear father has just been telling me that wedding plans are progressing more rapidly than you orignally planned. You shall be a bride long before spring is out. Why, it is quite exciting, isn't it, Eleanor?"

"Thank you," Beth mumbled as Nell muttered her agreement.

"Mr. Trant has told me how anxious the groom is," Drusilla continued as she lavishly spread honey on a thick slice of bread, "and I cannot but feel it is a good sign for your marriage. Has the actual date been settled upon yet?"

The Trant sisters were saved from having to answer by their father's gruff intervention. "Humph, humph! Not yet, m'dear Miss Poole, not yet. Humph! But we'll have it set before the day's out."

"We will?" put in Beth, blanching to the shade of the linen tablecloth.

"Didn't I just say so?" her father returned on a slight huff. "I'm to see Grayson this evening to settle the matter. He wants to announce the wedding day when he puts out the news of your betrothment tomorrow night."

Following this astonishingly lengthy speech, Mr. Trant retreated behind his coffee cup and morning paper, leaving the discussion to the ladies. This, unfortunately, did not make for a great deal of conversation. Beth had given up even the pretense of eating, while Nell sat staring into her teacup as if transfixed by the liquid inside it. Meanwhile, Miss Poole selected her second slice of bread and seemed extraordinarily cheerful.

"I am to go to Lombard Street this afternoon to book that seat on the Mail," she said. "Did you wish to come with me, Eleanor?"

"What? Uh, no." Nell had no wish to be reminded further of her departure, but saw the quizzical lift of Drusilla's thin brows and offered lamely, "I have quite a deal to do to finish before tomorrow night, you know."

"Ah, yes, the ball. How you must be looking forward to it, Elizabeth," she added before biting into her honeyed bread.

Suddenly Beth leapt up, sending her chair flying. "I— I'm sorry! It's just that—that I've remembered dozens of things that m-must be d-done!" she spluttered as she dashed from the room.

"What the deuce's got into that chit?" demanded Mr. Trant, snapping his paper back into position before his nose.

Without answering, Nell made her excuses and fled after her sister. All her earlier spirits had been crushed with the morning's disclosures, and she now needed some vigorous activity to revive them.

She found it in the kitchen. After pounding bread dough with such vehemence that the cook feared for the outcome of the buns, Nell progressed to making a cake. She was in the midst of zealously whisking a spoon through a bowl, scattering drops without heed, when Fowles coughed behind her.

"Well, what is it?" she demanded without missing a stroke.

"You have a caller, Miss. Lord Warwynne awaits you in the sitting room."

Her fierce scowl sent the servant away with a shake of his head, but she clapped the bowl down to the tabletop, spilling large quantities of batter, and followed him. Her hair, which she'd put up neatly this morning, now tumbled haphazardly from its knot around her heat-flushed face. She had not removed the apron she had donned in the kitchen and so presented Viscount Warwynne with a bespattered, befloured image. He gazed at her in open-mouthed amazement until she snapped, "Well? I haven't all day, Arthur. What do you want?"

"I, that is to say, uh—"

"For heaven's sake, speak out!"

"D'you *always* look like this at home?" he asked, his mouth finally closing.

His question was so unexpected that for a moment Nell was taken aback. Then, looking down at her smeared apron, she realized what a sight she must present, and her impotent anger vanished in a flood of humor. Shocking the viscount still more, she burst into laughter, laughing harder when she caught sight of herself in the circular convex mirror. While Lord Warwynne stood by helplessly, she gripped her sides and panted with near-hysteria. Her hair! Her face! No wonder he was looking at her as if she were mad!

Finally she collapsed onto the jade settee and wiped the tears from her eyes, feeling relieved of the tension she'd sought to release in baking. Studying his lordship as she calmed herself, she could not help smiling. If he had called to restate his petition for her hand, he clearly no longer desired to do so. Seeing her for the first time as something other than the magnificent goddess he had always thought her, the veils had been lifted from his eyes. Nell could not help feeling a little sorry for him and for herself because of it, so she smiled kindly at him and gestured for him to be seated.

"Please forgive me, Arthur. But I looked *such* a sight! I admire you for not laughing at me when I entered."

"Oh, no, I would not, I could not—"

"But of course you wouldn't! You are quite the kindest gentleman I know. But I ask your forgiveness for my intemperate, untidy entrance just the same. I've been under quite a strain recently, but that gives me no right to act in an ill-bred manner toward you." She saw him color up and changed to a crisper tone. "Now tell me, if you will, why you wished to see me."

He looked relieved and managed a smile of his own.

"The thing is, Nell, I've struck upon a way to raise the wind for you. I knew I should, given the chance."

She frowned, confused. "Raise the—you mean, to get the twenty thousand pounds for me?"

"Yes, dash it! I knew we weren't basketed, not while I still had a bit of the ready."

His boyish enthusiasm brought her to her feet in a joyous leap. "But how? Where? Do you have it now?"

"Well, no, not yet," he admitted. As her face fell, he went on swiftly, "But we shall have it today, I assure you. Can you come out with me now?"

"Oh, I—yes! Yes, I can! Wait for me!" As she raced upstairs to throw off her apron and old gown, it occurred to Nell that she still had not the least idea by what means Lord Warwynne had raised the funds. But she did not really care so long as she had it to hand to Sir Charles before tomorrow night's announcement. She would, of course, be repaying the viscount for the rest of her life and could never now be free from her school, but none of that mattered as long as Beth had the chance for happiness that she herself had lost.

Grabbing at random from her mahogany wardrobe, Nell pulled on her pine-green merino dress without even seeing what she put on. Without brushing a curl, she stuffed her hair beneath her green-sashed chip bonnet, then pulled on a fringed shawl and her short kid gloves as she descended to the sitting room. Lord Warwynne seemed as impatient as she, and they were off the instant she appeared.

It was not until they had passed the limits of the city, seated side-by-side in his lordship's curricle, that Nell at last wondered where they were going. Her mind had been thoroughly taken up with visions of Sir Charles's face when she coolly presented him with twenty thousand pounds and bade him to cease forcing himself upon her family. But when she noticed they were coming upon Putney Heath, Nell started from her pleasant reflections and desired Lord Warwynne to tell her what they were doing so far from Town.

"We're going to collect our winnings, Miss Trant," he replied with a ready smile.

A feeling of dread stole over her, but she beat it back

and inquired as calmly as she could, "But whatever do you mean, Arthur? What winnings?"

"Our twenty thousand pounds, of course," he said in surprise. He briefly cast his soulful eyes upon her, then returned his attention to his team as he turned them onto a little-traveled, poorly marked country road. "When Fancy Lady comes in, we must be there to pocket the blunt!"

"Do you mean—can you possibly mean to say that we are going to a *race?*" Nell demanded in an ominously quiet tone.

"Well, of course," he replied. "What else did you think?"

"I thought," she said, "that we were doing something other than wasting my time!"

"No, but—"

"Have the goodness to turn around and bring me home," Nell requested with icy hauteur.

"But, Eleanor, it's a certain thing, I assure you. We've as good as got the ready in our hands," his lordship protested. "When I won at Brook's yesterday night, it all but fell into our laps. Fancy Lady's running at fifty-to-one—"

"Fifty to one! And you expect to *win?*"

"—and with just four hundred pounds, we can have our twenty thousand before the day is out," Warwynne concluded animatedly. "I knew it was meant to be when my button came off my waistcoat and—"

"We are going to God-knows-where on the basis of a *button?* Take me home, my lord!"

"I'm telling you, fate sent this to us. My button rolled onto an announcement of this race and landed right on Fancy Lady's name. Surely you must see what that means!"

"I see, Lord Warwynne, that it means you are more harebrained than even I believed possible!" Nell snapped, her dreams turning to dust even as the hooves of his lordship's team kicked that commodity up into her face. "I demand that you turn around now. I've no intention of seeing this race or any other."

"Dash it all!" he expostulated, turning an angry face to her. "This isn't some nodcock notion, you know!"

Even as he spoke, his tiger seated behind him shouted, "Look out, m'lord!"

Startled, Nell looked up in time to see a four-in-hand

coach bearing down upon them. Warwynne pulled on the reins, but in his agitation he was too forceful and his horses reared up, rending the air with their whinnying protest. The next instant, as the coach flashed past them, an appalling crunch of splintering wood sounded, and they were jolted roughly from their seats and thrown to the ground.

Several stunned seconds later Nell opened her eyes to darkness. The instant of panic left her as she pushed the brim of her bonnet back from her face and rose shakily to her feet, fixing a wrathful eye upon his lordship.

"Now see what you have done!" she exclaimed, pointing an accusing finger at the curricle, which lay on its side, bereft of one bright yellow wheel.

# - 14 -

THE AFTERNOON HAD given way to evening by the time Miss Trant and Lord Warwynne ceased blaming one another for the accident. While his lordship maintained that Miss Trant's arguing had distracted him, she held that his own lack of sense was responsible. Words of accusation and condemnation had flown thickly, clouding common sense from view until Warwynne's tiger pointed out that the horses must be released from their traces. The young groom had been the most severely injured, with a nasty cut upon his forehead, but he declared himself able and willing to ride for help on one of the horses, which he did as soon as the animals were freed.

He left the pair behind him sunk in gloom, rousing themselves only to cast further slurs upon each other's head. They nearly came to blows when Lord Warwynne declared he could now see why his mother had said Miss Trant would never get off the shelf, but would remain an old maid. In the end, however, Nell merely sniffed and sat down in the grass at the roadside where the lone horse now grazed.

Stripping off her gloves, she uprooted handfuls of green grass, spilling them indiscriminately over her lap. Finally she lay back in the cool grass and studied the loitering progress of white clouds across the clear sky while counting to herself in an effort to regain her temper. The fresh scent of the new grass, the lazy caress of the late afternoon sun, and the rhythmic swish of the horse's tail all lulled Nell into a pleasant sleep.

When she awoke, it was chill and silent. She was cramped and sore, and it was rapidly nearing nightfall. She sat up with a jerk, then sprang to her feet as she realized with a pounding heart that the bay was gone. Lord Warwynne had deserted her!

Her fear turned to sheer fury. Nell strode to the road and stood uncertainly for a bare moment before beginning to walk back in the direction of Town. She kicked a ball of dust at his lordship's curricle as she passed it and thought how pleasurable it would be to kick him instead. *Men!* she thought with keen hostility. They were all the same. And not worth a tuppence the lot. If she could but lay her hands on one of them . . .

Her vexation gave her the energy to keep walking long after she was too tired to do so. As darkness wrapped itself about her, she was forced to step more cautiously, stumbling several times and tripping once on the hem of her skirt. At last she thought she could move no farther. Too weary to maintain even her anger, she sank to the roadside and considered crying. She was, she decided, fatigued beyond tears.

A distant drumming caught her attention. As it neared, it crystallized into the hammering of horses' hooves and the creak of wheels along the road. Her heart matching the beat of the horses' gait Nell stood to the side and waited, ready to hail the vehicle and beg for aid. But she had no need to stop the carriage for, as the old country gig drawn by a slump-backed nag drew up, it pulled to a halt. Looking up, she was amazed to discover Lord Warwynne handling the ribbons.

"Miss Trant! I feared I should not get back before you awoke. I trust you did not suffer undue alarm?" He held a hand down to her, which she accepted silently as he rattled on, "When Toby didn't return, I could wait no longer. I took off after him, and it's a deuced good thing I did! That bump to his head was worse than we thought. He fell from his horse and I found him lying by the side of the road. But

I plucked him up and went on to procure this gig."

Feeling suddenly too tired to care whether she might have been murdered or worse while left alone by the side of the road, Nell made no comment whatsoever during the return journey, contenting herself with merely staring dully at the blue-black sky. When his lordship drew up before her home and tried to make an impassioned apology, she waved him away with one hand, expressed her hope that Toby was quite recovered, and bade him goodnight. She felt as utterly ramshackle as she knew she must appear and desired only to retire to her room.

Entering the foyer, she left a trail of dust from the torn hem of her long skirt. Fortunately, the grass stains could not be easily seen on the dark green of her gown, but the stains upon her hands stood out vividly, as did the dirt beneath her nails. Her hair, which had not been properly combed to start, tumbled in bedraggled snarls about her shoulders. Her bonnet, with its soiled, crumpled sash, hung limply from her hand, and her shawl dragged from elbow to elbow in twisted disarray. Thus it was not to be wondered at that Miss Poole stopped dead upon sighting this raga-muffin vision.

"Eleanor! What on earth has happened?" she cried. "As if there has not already been enough!"

"It is nothing, Drusilla. Do not fuss. Indeed, Lord War-wynne's curricle met with an accident, but nothing is truly the matter that a little soap and water cannot mend. You need not look so distraught."

"But you do not know!" Drusilla objected. Lowering her voice to a dramatic whisper, she explained, "I've been wait-ing for *hours* to tell you! You must come with me at once!"

She did not listen to Nell's loud protests, but clasped her hand and tugged her into the sitting room. Shutting the door, she leaned against it and said with uncharacteristic emotion, "I have been out of my mind with worry! I fear I do not know what is to be done!"

In no mood to face such theatrics, Nell sagged where she stood and said with a heavy sigh, "Drusilla, I beg you to cease enacting me a tragedy and tell me what is wrong. I've had the most distressful day and long only for a bath and my bed."

"I scarce know where to begin," Drusilla declared, wringing her hands. "You see, I had the misfortune of being in a most awkward position this afternoon."

"Please cease this roundaboutation!" Nell begged. Her voice hovered in the air, then tumbled tiredly as she dropped upon the nearest chair.

Miss Poole took the opposite chair, folded her hands together, inhaled deeply, and began. "Very well. Your sister Elizabeth received a call from Mr. Perkins this afternoon here in the sitting room. I had come to this room to be by the warmth of the fire and was employing my time by mending several unmentionables when I heard them approach. Upon recognizing the deep tones of a male voice, I naturally repaired behind the screen to avoid the embarrassment that must ensue should he see the articles upon which I worked."

Both ladies focused upon the cloth print screen standing in the farthest corner of the room. Knowing why Beth had invited Mr. Perkins to call, Nell said simply, "You overheard them."

"I *meant* to make my presence known immediately. But before I could—the very instant the door had shut, in fact— Elizabeth behaved in the most shocking manner!" Miss Poole's indignation pealed through the room. "She threw herself upon the gentleman most wantonly and professed her love for him! And she addressed him by his Christian name!"

Nell brightened. At last some good news! Eagerly, she leaned toward her friend and demanded to know Mr. Perkins's response to this disgraceful behavior.

"At first he acted quite properly. He detached your sister from about his neck and begged she would remember she was about to become affianced to another. But I'm afraid Elizabeth was lost to all sense of propriety. She promptly flung herself back into his arms and announced she did not care for anything but *him!*"

Better and better. Nell's fatigue fell away with the thrill of success, and she prompted impatiently, "And then? What happened then?"

"Oh, my dear, I cannot know how to tell you," Drusilla claimed on a near-wail. "Elizabeth told the gentleman—my dear, you will never credit this, I'm sure—she told him that *you* had fallen in love with him and desired to be his wife."

Striving to keep from betraying herself with a blush, Nell bent her head and murmured, "Where can she have gotten such a caper-witted notion?"

"I need not tell you that Mr. Perkins was horror-stricken at that idea! And then, oh, Eleanor, and then your sister descended to such vulgarity I know not how to tell you!"

"Just tell me, Drusilla. You only make it worse by all this rambling."

"They discussed what to do that would cause the least suffering for everyone, the least scandal, and all the while Beth insisted that if you wish to marry him, you would, for no one was more determined than you—with which, Eleanor, I can only agree, for you are very like a dog with a bone once you—"

"Dru! What did they decide?" broke in Nell with a great deal of heat. This was what she had been working toward— Beth's decision to end her betrothment to Sir Charles—and she must hear of it now!

"My dear, they've run off!" cried Miss Poole.

For a moment Nell did not understand. "Run off?" she repeated stupidly.

"Eloped!"

"What!"

With the satisfaction of one who has delivered a piece of news to great effect, Miss Poole explained, "As bold as brass, Elizabeth declared they should elope. To give him credit, Mr. Perkins strenuously resisted the idea at first, but your sister convinced him it was the only way. She told him you would come to understand and forgive him in time and that it would be far better to break swiftly and cleanly than to prolong your suffering. I do not know how I remained silent behind the screen."

The fog of stupefaction was clearing. Nell shook her head, then stood up. "When did all this occur? Have they already left? Have you told anyone else?"

"No," Dru replied in response to the last of these rapid volleys. "Your parents have been from home since early afternoon and neither has returned. Mr. Perkins left, then returned at five o'clock. Elizabeth went with him."

"Five o'clock! It is nearing nine now! You did nothing to stop them?"

"My dear, what could I do? I have no say over your sister's actions."

With another emphatic shake of her head, Nell cleared the last of the shock from her mind. She had never meant for Beth to go to such scandalous lengths. They must be stopped before the story was out. Ignoring Drusilla's questions, Nell ran from the room, heading straight for the morning room. There she threw open the desk and did not pause before gripping paper and quill.

Though she had determined never to speak to him again following the argument at Almack's, Nell did not hesitate now. Hastily, she scribbled, *Come at once. I need you. Nell.* Smudging the words as she folded the paper without allowing the ink to dry, she dashed out, calling for Fowles as she went. The instant he appeared, she instructed him to deliver the note immediately to Sir Charles. "Search the town for him if you must, but get this into his hands as quickly as possible!" she ordered.

Moving directly to her room, she scrubbed the grime from her hands and face, pulled her hair back into a loose knot, and was reaching for the first button of her gown when Drusilla burst in to tell her that Mrs. Trant had arrived home at last. Leaving the button, she snatched up her heavy cloak and draped it over one arm as she strode into her mother's boudoir, preparing herself for what could only be an exhausting interview with Mama.

To Eleanor's vast surprise, her mother received the news of her younger daughter's elopement with astonishing calm. She reclined on her chaise longue with closed eyes and merely wondered on a long sigh, "Whatever can have gotten into the silly child that she must needs run away like this?"

Perversely, her mother's placid acceptance sent Nell flying up into the boughs again. "What can have got into her? I can tell you, Mama, precisely what! Who wouldn't run off to get away from being forced into marriage!"

"Such fustian, Eleanor," her mother said without moving a hair. "No one was forcing Beth into marriage. And it appears, my child, that marriage is precisely what your sister is after."

"But not to Sir Charles! I cannot say that I blame Beth

in the least!" Nell declared, pacing back and forth as she ranted on. "Oh, I'm not saying that we shall allow her to make such a mistake as a Gretna Green marriage. We shall stop her. But I don't wonder at her going to such lengths to avoid a life with Sir Charles Grayson and all his mistresses."

Mrs. Trant opened one eye, watched her daughter take one fervent turn about the carpet, shuddered and closed it again. "*Must* you move so . . . energetically?" she inquired plaintively. After a brief silence, she lifted her lids again to see Nell leaning wearily against the fireplace mantel, her bent head pressed into her crossed forearms. "You should not say such foolish things, you know Eleanor."

The head lifted and Nell fixed a tired eye upon her. "What do you mean?"

"My dear child, everyone knows the baronet hasn't kept any muslin company in the last three years."

"He hasn't?" Nell stared at her mother in disbelief. "But—but what about Alicia Alverton?"

"Alicia Alverton has been the companion of the Marquess of Strathe these past three years and more," her mother answered.

"And more?" Nell repeated sharply, every muscle in her face taut with tension. It could not—it simply could not be the truth. She *knew* he had seen Alicia on the day of their betrothment—or at least, she *thought* he had. She had no time to sort out her memories, however, for Fowles entered with a sharp tap to announce that Sir Charles was waiting for them below.

Nell did not stop to think how she should greet the man with whom she had so recently and so violently argued. She swept up her cloak and took the stairs at a gallop. He stood in the hall, quizzically watching her flying descent. She was aware of a tremendous relief and without hesitation came to a halt by casting herself into the folds of his greatcoat and exclaiming, "Thank God you have come!"

Clamped as she was against his chest, Nell felt the shudder that passed through him. She heard the breath he drew from his innermost depths and quivered in trembling response. His arms came round to enfold her for the barest second, then his hands took firm hold of her shoulders, and he put her from him. Tilting her white face up to the light of the branched candelabra, he searched her eyes intently.

"What is wrong, Nell? How may I be of help to you?"

His controlled tones calmed her and, taking a steadying breath, she opened her mouth to reply. But it merely hung wordlessly wide as she took in the bright hint of a snowy cravat at his neck, the tight black trousers flowing into pumps at his feet. Contrition furrowed her brow. "Oh," she said flatly, "you're wearing evening dress."

"Yes. I was on my way out when your note arrived." His lips curved gravely upward. "And it looks rather as if *you've* been out. What has happened? Why are you looking like some street ragamuffin?"

"I'm sorry," she murmured with unaccustomed penitence. "I've had a rather . . . distressful day. I shouldn't have disturbed your evening."

"Don't be cloth-headed, Nell," he returned softly. "If you needed me, I would come from the gates of heaven to help you. Now tell me why you summoned me so frantically."

She managed a lopsided smile. "It's Beth. She's eloped. With Mr. Perkins."

His hands dropped away from her arms and his brow lifted. "Indeed?"

"Yes! We—we must go after them, stop them before it's too late!" The emotional strain of the day became a burden Nell could no longer bear. Before she could repress them, tears welled up in her eyes to spill over her lashes, clumping them darkly together. They coursed in rivulets down her cheeks, one charting a path over her nose. She made no effort to stop them or to dash them away, but let them stream freely down to splash past the fluted lace about her neck to form dark patches on the bodice of her dress.

Sir Charles did not attempt to interrupt her weeping, but began issuing orders like a general about to enter the battlefield. He dispatched his groom with commands to return with the baronet's curricle and fleetest team of horses, as well as a sturdy pair of boots and leather gloves. He sent Fowles to fill a flask with Mr. Trant's best brandy. Even Miss Poole was recruited to request a light, quick meal of the cook. When they were alone in the hall, he turned at last to Nell and said in a voice that was oddly rough, "Don't worry, Nell, I'll have them back well before dawn. In a hired chaise they can't be too far ahead."

Nell sniffed, then hiccuped. She rubbed her dampened face vigorously with both palms, then sniffed again. Through her fingers she saw a fluttering of white, reached gratefully for the proffered handkerchief, and blew her nose with a most unladylike thoroughness. At last she expelled a deep sigh. "Thank you. You are very . . . kind."

Sir Charles ignored this compliment, taking his balled kerchief and stuffing it into his pocket in silence. Each action seemed to Nell to be filled with a new poignancy, and she found herself unable to look at him. The intricate scrolls of the marble side table assumed an absorbing interest to her. Tracing the swirls of the marble with one finger, she studied the scrolls while inquiring, "How soon do you think we shall be able to leave?"

"We, Nell? I rather think I shall be off within the hour," Sir Charles replied with the suggestion of a smile.

Opposition was ever the meat of life to Nell. She threw her head up, met his blue gaze squarely, and stated firmly, "Of course I am going with you, Sir Charles. Beth is, after all, my sister. I shall be needed to accord her chaperonage."

"It may be hours before I catch up with them—hours in an open curricle, stopping only to change horses. I cannot possibly allow you to accompany me on such a journey."

"Allow! I am not seeking your permission, Sir Charles. I am insisting that I come with you. If you do not wish for me to ride in your curricle, very well, I shall hire a coach and go after them myself. Which is what I should have done in the first place," she finished with a snap.

"I believe, Sir Charles," said another, unexpected voice, "that you should accept her companionship, if it will not put you out too much to do so."

The pair in the hall whirled to gaze upward at Mrs. Trant, who graced the head of the staircase. At the same instant, Drusilla returned, followed by Fowles, bearing a tray stacked with thick slices of heavy bread, slabs of meat and cheese, a mug of ale and one slim pewter flask. Sir Charles shot an impatient glance over them, then turned back to stare up at Mrs. Trant. His eyes narrowed and the muscles in his cheek flexed before he brought his gaze to rest briefly on Nell's tense, determined face.

"Have you eaten?" he asked brusquely.

"No, but I'm not the least hungry," she returned.

"Nonetheless, I suggest that you join me in a quick meal. This isn't a pleasure outing, Miss Trant, and you'll need the strength of solid food before we're through."

He turned on his heel and strode into the breakfast room. By the time Nell joined him, he had pieced together a quick sandwich and was into his second bite. Sitting as far away from him as possible, she likewise put meat and cheese between bread and forced herself to eat. Words floated through the open doorway as her mother and Miss Poole entered.

"But I cannot feel that it would be right for her to do so," Drusilla was saying in strident tones that conveyed the depth of her opposition.

"You must, of course, feel whatever you choose to, Miss Poole." Mrs. Trant sighed as she subsided onto an embroidered chair cushion. "If you have no other choice but to object to this venture, I beg you will make your wishes known to someone else."

"Of course I object to it! Any person of sensibility would!" Miss Poole pronounced. Facing Nell, she stretched her hand across the table. "My dear, you must not let your emotions run away with you. if you will but consider a moment, you will see that it is both unnecessary and unwise for you to accompany Sir Charles."

Nell retrieved a stray crumb from her lip with the tip of her tongue before responding. "I am going, Drusilla, and that is that. Someone must be there to protect Beth's reputation."

Arrested by the force of this argument, Miss Poole sat very still, then slowly drew back her hand. Taking a sidelong look at the baronet, she ventured, "Perhaps I could go along . . ."

"My curricle will be damnably overcrowded and weighted to the speed of syrup as it is, Miss Poole," Sir Charles maintained between bites. "I fear you shall have to remain here and pray I don't ravish Miss Trant upon the road."

"Really, sir!" Miss Poole exclaimed, in the same breath begging Nell to reconsider.

"Whichever it is, Miss Trant had best decide now," the baronet said, rising. As he took a pair of high-topped boots from Fowles, he sat on the nearest chair and quickly stripped off his pumps, replacing them with the boots. "Either she is coming or not, but I am leaving on the instant."

"Oh, please, wait!" Nell cried. She, too, had risen and now stood half in her cloak and half out, struggling with the bulk of the heavy material. "I need my—my hat and things."

Without glancing in her direction, Sir Charles donned his caped greatcoat and pocketed the flask. Striding out, he barked curtly, "I give you one minute, Nell, not a second more."

As Nell scrambled from behind the table, Fowles held out her sadly rumpled chip bonnet and a small reticule. A smile of gratitude lit her face before she dashed down the hall in Sir Charles's shadow. He halted abruptly, and she crashed into his back as her mother's voice wafted after to them.

"Sir Charles, I trust you to resolve this matter," Mrs. Trant said in a voice threaded with what Nell thought to be unnatural humor. "Once and for all," she added cryptically, just as the baronet caught hold of Nell's arm and dragged her out into the night.

# - *15* -

THE NIGHT CLOUDS clung together, obscuring all view of the moon and stars. Sir Charles stared up at the sky with a frown as he drew on his gloves. Nell noted his abstraction and, setting her hand lightly on his arm, asked quietly, "Do you think we stand the least chance of catching them?"

His head swung down as if only now remembering her presence. "I would not set out if I did not think so. Come, get you up and let us be off or we shan't have our chance, after all."

Placing his hands on her slim waist, he lifted her easily to the seat of his curricle, then climbed up beside her. Taking the reins in one hand and his whip in the other, he nodded to his groom, who instantly released the leaders' heads. The curricle shot away so quickly that Nell feared the groom would not make his leap onto the perch behind them, but he did so quite nimbly and they were off through the city streets.

Though she had traveled these thoroughfares many times, during both day and night, this time everything seemed imbued with a vivid animation, as if the whole of London were aware of her adventure. As their curricle weaved in and out of the traffic, street lamps burst by them with the brightness of fireworks and the most minor noises exploded in Nell's over-sensitive ears. Gradually the bustle of townlife faded into a quiet rustic calm, and she let loose a long sigh and ceased to grip her reticule so tightly.

Sir Charles noted her slight movement and darted one quick glance at her. Returning his eyes to the gray ribbon of visible road, he asked, "Where are your gloves?"

"I—well, I lost them today and did not think to get another pair out," Nell stumbled. She watched the pale silhouette of his profile tighten and thought she heard the word "damnation" drift through the brisk air, but she could not be certain.

That was the extent of their conversation for several miles as the baronet was forced to concentrate on keeping to the darkened road, only narrowly missing two very nasty ruts and once taking a sharp turn within an inch of a sunken ditch. Nell's thoughts rambled from admiration for such skilled handling of a four-in-hand to castigation of herself for Beth's current predicament. In the midst of telling herself precisely how wrongly she had behaved with regard to Mr. Perkins, she realized that the curricle had slowed and was, indeed, stopping. Looking about her, she saw that they had entered the cobbled yard of a posting inn. She inquired of Sir Charles where they were.

"Barnet," he answered shortly. "We're not stopping beyond time to refresh the horses, so don't get down."

She had no opportunity to disabuse him of such notions, for he vaulted down and, together with his groom, rapidly watered his team. As they worked, the clouds graciously parted to allow patches of moonlight to streak the earth. When they were off again, Nell felt Sir Charles's tension ease and sent a small thank you up to the sky.

Just then Sir Charles startled her by suddenly requesting, "Explain to me, if you will, how all this came about."

Hoping the speckled moonlight did not permit him to see her blush, Nell began in an unusually meek voice. "Well, you see, I discovered quite some time ago that Beth ...cherished a certain...regard for Mr. Perkins and—"

"So that explains it!"

"Explains what?" she asked. Peering at him through the shadows, she could only just see the sneering tilt of his lips.

"Your sudden...attraction—shall we say?—for Mr. Perkins."

The weight of that harsh truth bowed Nell's head. From beneath her bonnet, her words rushed breathlessly out into the night. "Yes. Well, I did not think it . . . right for Beth to—to marry you when she loved him, so I—"

"So you interfered," he cut in with a voice that echoed his whip cracking overhead. "Tell me, my dear, have you been taking lessons on meddling from your dear Miss Poole?"

"My interference was at least preferable to your indifference! You don't care a fig for Beth!" Nell flared, her head lifting in sudden defiance.

"I care enough to see that her reputation is not damaged from this tangle you have made," he responded through clenched lips.

"*I* have made! Why—"

"I am interested in knowing, Miss Trant," he went on as if she had not spoken, "precisely how you led them to elope."

"I did not lead them to it! Indeed, I never meant—"

"No? But what then did you mean? Did you hope for a scene tomorrow night to ridicule me? One very like the last one you contrived?"

His mocking anger had a curious effect on her. Her temper rose, leaping in flames to lick fiercely at his accusations. But since she had spent the last few hours heaping blame upon herself for having brought her sister to such a pass, Nell also recognized the justness of the baronet's scornful words, and that recognition shot through her with the shattering intensity of a bullet through paper.

"No," she whispered, turning her head so that he could see only a vague outline of her face. She searched for words to explain to him without also revealing her aching love and found none. So she sat clutching her reticule in her wind-chafed hands, miserably aware of the hard muscles so close to hers, the strong movements of the arm beside hers as it guided the reins.

Obviously he despised her for her part in tonight's muddle and, indeed, she could not blame him for it. She despised herself. Sinking lower and lower into a pool of self-pity, she began to feel each bump and twist of the ride. It seemed to her she had spent a lifetime being jostled about in curricles. Her back ached abominably and she felt jolted out of her skin, while her cheeks and hands stung from the constant cruel caress of the wind. She refused, however, to give Sir Charles the satisfaction of an uttered complaint and forced herself to sit straighter still in mute discomfort.

As they pulled into the next posting inn, Nell realized that her weariness following her earlier misadventure had been like a single grain of sand on a beach. Now she knew what it was to feel totally exhausted, both physically and mentally. Her secret relief when Sir Charles explained that they would be stopping here to change horses was immense. He came round to her side of the curricle and stretched out his arms to her. She hesitated, saw him scowl, then leaned forward and let him lift her to the ground. Her legs were stiff, her first step unsteady, and somehow Nell found herself leaning into the support of the baronet's broad shoulder, his arm around her back.

Despite her fatigue such intimate contact instantly awakened her senses. Through the heavy materials of his coat and hers, she felt the warmth of his arm like a brand searing into her back. The steady thumping of his heart assaulted her ear where her head lay against his chest, and the scent of starch wafted up from his cravat to tickle her nose. She watched the gravel crunch beneath their feet while tasting the crisp night air as it lay upon her tongue. Ridiculously, she wished this moment could last forever.

It did not do so, of course, and within minutes she was settled on a cushioned bench, her hands and feet held out to a roaring blaze that crackled and popped. Sir Charles had disappeared to oversee the selection of a fresh team, but had thoughtfully ordered a cup of steaming tea for her. As the pot-bellied landlord handed it to her with a cheery, "This'll put a spot o'color in yer cheeks, missy!", she produced a wretched smile. Slowly she removed both her cloak and bonnet and lay them on the bench beside her.

Taking an exploratory sip of the hot tea, she tucked her feet up beneath the torn hem of her gown and stared into the flames. Sorting the blue ones from the red, the red from the white, Nell attempted to make sense of what her mother had told her earlier. If, in truth, Sir Charles had ceased to keep Alicia Alverton before their engagement, she had done him a gross injustice. And, she thought sadly, ruined her own chance for happiness. It didn't bear thinking of. She set down her cup and placed her hands at the small of her back, trying to ease the cramping pain and striving not to think.

"You must forgive me my earlier temper, Miss Trant," said a voice behind her.

Her hands flew out from her back, knocking over the cup and spilling its contents over her bonnet and cloak. Nell jumped up and grabbed her cloak. As she yanked it up, however, the teacup descended from its folds to the floor with a crash. A firm hand moved her to the side. Then Sir Charles was bending to pick up fragments of broken china.

"It seems I am ever startling you, Nell. I shall learn in future to announce myself with greater care."

She watched the fire's radiant glow dance over his glossy black curls bent so near to it, and her breath caught tightly in her throat. She felt as if her voice had been captured in the grip of an unknown hand. She could not speak, though her mind fairly burst with words—of apology, forgiveness, agony and love, all unspoken, all unheard.

Sir Charles stood up, dumped the shards onto the saucer, and moved to set the saucer on a round table in one corner of the small parlor. Nell focused on the outward swirl of his long, dark coat, trying vainly to ignore the supple grace of his movements. As he returned to stand before her, the agonizing battering of her heart against her ribs commanded all of her attention, but slowly she became aware of the frown gathering in his deep blue eyes and a question came into her own.

"You look worn to your back teeth, my dear," he said, his voice devoid of the concern his words expressed. "Your eyes are more heavily shadowed than the sky, and the only color I can see comes where the firelight strikes your copper hair." He paused as if expecting her to argue. When she said nothing, continuing only to stand staring at him with wide eyes, he went on in a voice grown suddenly husky. "You cannot possibly continue on, Nell. I think you should stay here in Welwyn. I'll collect you on the way back. You'll be able to rest and still provide the necessary chaperonage for Beth into Town."

That at last penetrated her benumbed state. She would *not* be left behind! She reclaimed her voice from the unknown hand and protested angrily, "I'll do no such paltry thing! I don't need to be wrapped in swaddling!"

She had intended the words to come ringing forcefully out and she was humiliated to discover that her voice was a feeble thread. Still she tried to maintain her point by glaring at Sir Charles.

In one grim stride, he was before her, her shoulders clamped relentlessly in his hands. Shaking her until the loose knot of her hair gave way to spill curls over his whitened knuckles, he demanded irately, "Will you never listen to reason? Will you never use the least sense? Damnation, Nell, must you ever oppose me?"

Of a sudden he stopped shaking her. For an instant that seemed to Nell to burn away the years between them, he stood motionless, staring at her with eyes near-black with hunger. Then his palm came up to cradle her head, and his mouth came down to hers. From the fury and the passion within him, she expected a harsh, punitive kiss filled with rage. But his lips touched hers as lightly as fairy dust touches flower petals. They lingered, barely grazing her skin, as if he sought only to tempt her.

With a groan, the pent-up desires of three long, miserable years spilled forth, and Nell opened her lips against his, hungrily taking, seeking, tasting the warm moistness of his kiss. Her hands found their way into his hair, twining and twisting with a restless need. She fit her body into the contours of his and reveled in the shudder that shook him. She did not think or care where this would lead. She only knew that her heart was singing, soaring with fulfillment.

He moved his lips a breath away, while his hand gently stroked the line of her throat. "Oh, Nell, I love you. You must know how I love you."

Knowing he could feel the quickening of her pulse as it throbbed beneath his hand, she pulled slightly away. His hand, however, moved with her, thrilling her pulse to greater pounding.

"Love me?" she repeated on a ribbon of a sigh. "I thought you quite despised me."

The ghost of a laugh caressed her cheek. His tongue teased her lower lip. "God knows I've tried to. But you, my adorable firebrand, kept setting my resolve to flames." His lips moved to play with the lobe of her ear as he continued to murmur, "I meant to be cool and civil toward you, dear heart, but whenever we were alone, it was like this."

"Like this?" she asked lightly, nuzzling closer into the fine broadcloth of his greatcoat.

"Like this," he repeated. His finger traced the curve of her lips until they quivered for his kiss. "Every time I saw you, I could not keep my hands from you. I was driven mad with wanting you, Nell. I wanted to touch you, to kiss you." He suited action to words, sketching his mouth lightly over hers while his hands warmly framed her face, tilting her head back gently.

Then his tongue flicked her lips apart, and his kiss went deeper, deeper, probing and claiming with a feverish hunger. His hands pressed into her cheek bones until Nell thought they must surely snap. And all the while shiver after shiver rushed through her. Somewhere at the back of her mind it came to her that he had never kissed her like this before. If he had, she would have married him regardless of a hundred Alicia Alvertons! When at length he drew slightly away, Nell accused him breathlessly of stealing her soul with that kiss.

"We are even, then, my sweet," he said thickly into the curls tumbling above her ear, "for you consigned my soul to hell three years ago."

She leaned back to gaze up at him. The brilliancy of his blue eyes was dulled by the memory of pain, a pain that Nell knew well. Dropping her lashes against her cheek, she said ruefully, "But I was there beside you, Charles. I've thought of you gathering comfort in the arms of Alicia Alverton all these years. You can't conceive how tortured I've been."

Through the curtain of her lashes, she saw his mouth compress, his eyes harden. "Can't I? What do you suppose I've felt since the moment you flung her name at me at our ball, upbraiding me without justification?"

She raised her eyes. "But you didn't deny it."

"I was too angry to deny it. Angry and hurt beyond measure," he explained. Seeing incredulity pass over her face, he added with a bitter laugh, "Yes, I was hurt—deeply. It stung me to the depths that you would so readily accept Drusilla Poole's word without even asking me for the truth. You were so influenced by her that I couldn't stand the sight of her! I was jealous—jealous of a dried-up, ape-leading spinster!" He shook his head as if he could not yet believe it.

"She deserves better of you, Charles, truly she does," Nell said softly.

"Perhaps," he said shortly. Pressing close to him, she felt his heart beat against her own. He went on in a rough voice, "When you refused to hear my apologies, my explanations, I hated her for it. I knew her influence led you to choose the school over me. Then you went off to Norfolk with her."

His voice ended sharply, and Nell felt his pain as if it were her own. "Forgive me," she whispered into his shoulder. "Forgive me if you can."

She felt a burning as his lips trailed down her neck to the lace at her collar. She trembled as he moaned and his warm breath seeped beneath the lace. "If—if you will tell me now, my darling," she sighed even as a quiver of pleasure shook her, "I will know you truly forgive me."

For a moment she thought he would not speak, for his lips continued a slow pattern up the hollow of her neck and his hands delicately defined the outline of her bosom. Then his muscles tensed. Bending her head back, she looked into his hot gaze and an answering passion flared into her.

He gave a small shake as if to wake himself, then set her away from him. "I trust I shall not have to continue fighting my need for you much longer, my love."

His words confused her. She turned to face the fire and played nervously with the burnished ends of her hair. "But—but what are you saying?"

"My God, Nell!" he said sharply. He did not come closer, and she refused to look at him. "I mean that I am tired of having to act the gentleman around you," he stated starkly. "Tired of having to hide my feelings for you. I want to do what we should have done three years ago. For God's sake, Nell, I want to marry you!"

She half-turned. Fire shadows dueled with firelight over the lines of her face, concealing her expression in their conflict. The bodice of her dress moved in rapid agitation. "But what about Beth?" she asked in a voice that carefully concealed her emotion.

"You can't seriously believe I ever meant to marry Beth."

At that Nell faced him on a whirl. "Of course you meant to! That is—didn't you?"

He moved a step closer, and she saw amusement glittering in his eyes. "Lord, no! You, my charming she-devil, are the only woman I've ever cared to wed."

"But—but—what were you up to, then?" she demanded, unwillingly sounding delighted.

"As soon as I heard that your father had gone aground, I bolted like a hare to ask for Beth. It occurred to me, you see, that the last thing you'd want was to have me for a brother-in-law." His smile teased her. "When you raced to Town to voice your opposition, I thought I'd found a way to get you back into my life at last." The smile twisted into self-mockery. "But I discovered you to be more of a devil's daughter than I'd counted on. You seemed to hate me more than ever, and I was torn between wanting to punish you and wanting to—"

"But if you didn't plan to marry Beth," Nell interrupted hurriedly, shying from the hungry need within his dark gaze, "then what did you intend for tomorrow night?"

His smile vanished altogether. His brows descended heavily. "I don't know. I was getting to the point where to have you as a sister was better than not having you at all. Several times I nearly threw away all my pride to beg you to listen . . . but each time that I lost control, you, my darling termagant, lost your temper. I feared you'd pack up and go back to that damned school. So I forced myself to hide my need, to pretend I wasn't shriveling up inside. When apology didn't work, I tried bribery."

Her brows rose. A hint of a laugh escaped him.

"Oh, yes," he confessed. "Your father's debts. I'd have paid considerably more than twenty thousand pounds to obligate you to me. I even thought of kidnapping you—though I had to drink the courage to contemplate it."

"The day I was leaving," Nell said with a sigh and saw the affirmation in his twinge of embarrassment. "And you were so rude to Drusilla because she spoiled your plans."

With wonder, Nell studied Charles as if seeing him for the first time—the thick black curls, the heavy brows standing in straight lines over his blinding blue eyes, the passionate mold of his lips. How could she have ever thought him arrogant or selfish? Though harsh, proud and strong, his face clearly bespoke his charm, his gentle kindness, his love.

"I've been the greatest beast!" she exclaimed. "I've been cruel and cold and mean and m-miserable! You can't p-possibly still wish to m-marry me!"

She was enfolded in his arms once more, his arms offering more than warmth and comfort. "I've no doubt you'll make me a very bad wife, Nellie, my love." He stifled her injured protest with a resounding kiss, breaking away to add softly at the edge of her lips, "But you're the only wife I'll ever want."

"I'll be forever losing my temper," she said, feeling she owed him a warning.

"I have always thought you magnificently lovely when angry, my firebrand," he said lightly.

She chanced a quick glance up at him and felt an unexpected surge of desire at the darkness within his lustrous eyes. He captured one copper ringlet and wound it around his finger, then leaned down to kiss the strand.

"Mmm, you smell of honeysuckle and springtime, Nell."

"I rather think I smell of dust," she returned in a blithe attempt to cover the power and depth of her tumultuous feelings. Her joy was such that it frightened her to admit it, as if to acknowledge her happiness would make it instantly vanish.

"That, too," he agreed easily. Slowly, he drew her toward the bench, and she found herself sitting within the circle of his arms, sighing contently while he catalogued her charms from head to toe. "Though when we are wed, my love," he finished in dulcet tones, "I shall endeavor to fatten you up. I'll not let you slip through my fingers again."

A tiny prick of pain punctuated her cloud of happiness. Studiously examining the oversized brass buttons of his coat, she said tentatively, "Could you tell me now, Charles, just what happened . . . before? I cannot think Drusilla would tell a deliberate lie."

His thumb and finger tipped her chin up. Her heart fitfully missed several beats as her eyes probed his. "She did not lie. I met with Alicia that day." His hand refused to allow her to look away. "But I did so only to sever the last of what had been a moribund relationship from the moment

I first saw you, Nell. You must believe that. Alicia had already gone to the protection of another—"

"The Marquess of Strathe," she supplied on a bare breath.

"Yes. But I owed Alicia much. She had been more giving than I in our relationship, and it would have been callous of me not to leave her some provision. I met her to give her the deed to a house in Town." He shrugged. "I've thought countless times that I should have sent my solicitor or my secretary or some other damn fool to give it to her—"

"No!" Nell said, sitting upright. "You did the most honorable and just thing. It is I who was the fool. And if you never forgive me, it would only serve me right!"

"Oh, my dear, dear, foolish Nell." He laughed, pulling her back into his embrace. "I love you."

# - 16 -

THE WIND HAD at last succeeded in chasing the clouds away, leaving the baronet's curricle in a bath of golden light upon the graveled courtyard. Nell eyed the vehicle with distaste and could not suppress a long-drawn sigh as Sir Charles lifted her up onto the seat.

"Are you too tired to make the journey, Nell? Shall we stay here the night and go on tomorrow?"

Moonbeams played tag over his upturned features. Looking down, Nell shook her head and saw the faintest frown pursue the streaks of light over his face. Then he turned and came round the curricle to climb in beside her. Before they set off, he tenderly placed a heavy laprobe over her legs and severely instructed her to keep her hands beneath its warmth.

"Yes, sir," she said most meekly.

He shot her a suspicious look, and she grinned in return. Laughing harmoniously, they left Welwyn behind. Happiness surged up within Nell until she felt she must release it or burst. Another deep sigh, this of contentment, rent the air.

"If you are weary, my dear, do not hesitate to lean upon me," said Sir Charles, keeping his eyes fixed on the road ahead of them.

"I am, rather," she confessed. Peeping up at him from around the edge of her bonnet, she inspected the lines of his face with a new shyness. "When this is over, I trust I shall never set foot in a curricle again. This afternoon's misadventures were quite enough alone without suffering the whole of the night in one as well."

"This afternoon?"

"Yes, I was out with Lord Warwynne," she began, then paused as she remembered why she had been with his lordship. "Well, um, well, we met with an accident and his wheel broke from his curricle and it was quite dreadful," she finished in a rush.

She took another peek around her bonnet and found to her dismay that a new severity had erased all the gentle lines from his face.

"I thought you were not encouraging the viscount," Sir Charles said tersely.

"I wasn't!" she immediately disclaimed. He threw her a disbelieving look before returning his gaze to the view beyond his team's head. "Truly, Charles! If—if you *must* know, his lordship was helping me . . . helping me to procure twenty thousand pounds."

This time the look he fastened on her was one of amazement, but she was relieved to note that the cold rigidity had yielded to a more relaxed warmth, and she quickly pressed her advantage. "You see, Charles—and I trust you will try to understand and not fly up into the boughs at me, for if you will remember, we were not on such good terms at that time—I meant to pay back the sum you settled on Papa and thus release Beth from her obligation to marry you."

She closed her eyes and held her breath, waiting for his explosion of scorn, his utter disgust of her. Her eyes flew open with the first crack of laughter and widened as he exclaimed, "You she-devil! The jealousies you put me through! I got the fright of my life the day I saw you and Warwynne exchanging what I thought were vows of love. How I wanted to murder him! Both of you! And now I find you were using him to settle your indebtedness to me. Just as you used Perkins to free Beth." His hand jerked slightly as he laughed, jolting the reins and sending the horses a series of confusing signals. Nell waited until he had steadied the team before responding and then she did so coolly.

"I did not *use* Lord Warwynne. At least," she conceded, "not at first. We failed to procure the funds, and in any case I do not see what you find so monstrously amusing."

"Don't you, my sweet?"

The clouds capriciously hid the moon and, as he returned his attention to keeping on the shadowed road, Nell did not prolong the argument. Little by little her body sagged more closely against the comforting support of his. She did not know when she dozed, or for how long, but at some point she ceased to be conscious of anything beyond her own contentment.

Something jarred her shoulder, her head lolled, and Nell suddenly became aware of bright lights and the buzz of voices around her. Raising her head from Sir Charles's caped shoulder, she saw before her sleep-fuzzed eyes the lamplit windows of a large, low building. Gradually, she focused on the activity in the midst of a cobbled courtyard—a grouping of ostlers and postboys around a well-weathered chaise.

"Awake, my darling?" whispered a tender voice.

Blushing with an inexplicable newfound shyness, Nell nodded to the baronet. "Where are we?" she inquired.

"Huntingdon—and, with any luck at all at the end of our chase."

"What?" Nell sat upright, suddenly awake.

"Unless what we hear about the overcrowding of the King's highways is more true than I'd previously believed, there aren't many hired coaches drawn by a single pair on the road at this time of night," Sir Charles explained, cocking his head toward the chaise in the yard.

As his groom ran to the hold the team's leaders, Sir Charles jumped down, then came to help Nell to the ground. This time as he lifted her down, his hands drifted slightly upward from her waist and lingered. His lips were but a whisper away from hers and her pulse throbbed violently. She forgot where they were, what they were doing there. Nell experienced a shuddering disappointment when, after bare seconds, he turned and led her through the doorway of the inn.

They stood in a wide, well-lit hallway with doors to either side of them and a staircase at the far end. A tall, stocky man with close-set eyes and the battered face of a pugilist materialized from a door beneath the stairs. Sir

Charles was about to address him when voices sailed out to the passageway.

"But we *must* go on," someone said in soggy tones.

"I cannot think it right," objected another, deeper voice. "We should turn back, my dear, you know we should."

"But I don't care about *shoulds!*" wailed the owner of the first voice.

Nell and Sir Charles looked at one another with triumph in their eyes, then turned as one toward the door to their right.

"Hold on! Where d'ye think ye're off to? That's a private room, already hired," protested the besmocked man from his stance by the stairs.

They did not so much as glance at him, but pushed wide the slightly ajar door to behold Elizabeth Trant sitting mournfully on a gilded wooden armchair with claw legs and bright red velvet upholstery which clashed with the deep pink of her round gown. Josiah Perkins stood before her, one arm stretched out, his short brown locks uncommonly disheveled. Both turned guiltily as the door swung open. A full view of puffed, reddened eyes and stained, full cheeks proclaimed Beth's distress while a tensed jaw evidenced Josiah's battle to maintain his usual self-control. This much Nell saw before her horrified sister cried out, "We are un-done!" and buried her head in her hands, bursting into fresh weeping.

Nell's aching fatigue vanished. She dashed to Beth's side and threw her arms about the young woman's trembling form.

"Beth, dearest! Of course you are not undone! Sir Charles and I are come to—"

"Oh, I know! I know!" Elizabeth bemoaned in a voice muffled by wrenching sobs. "You are come to return us to London and ruin our lives!" In one bound she thrust Nell's arms from her and pitched herself against the astounded Mr. Perkins. "D-don't let them do this to us, Josiah! T-tell them to b-be off!"

Mr. Perkins stared for a moment at the trembling pink and milk-white form crushing the knot of his cravat, then rose manfully to the occasion. "No one shall ruin your life, sweet Beth. I promise you that. No one," he repeated, glowering darkly at Sir Charles over the top of Beth's hair.

The implied threat in his scowl passed wide of its mark, for the baronet merely tipped his head and said mildly, "Quite right, Mr. Perkins. No one shall ruin Miss Beth's life—or yours."

The tangle of brown curls lifted slightly and a pair of shimmering eyes blinked at Sir Charles. "Do you mean you will not force us back to London?" Beth asked in quavering tones.

"I, my dear, would not think of forcing you to do anything," Sir Charles replied kindly.

"But you do see, don't you, dearest, that you must return to London?" put in Nell, with a quick, puzzled glance at the baronet.

"No," mumbled her sister into Mr. Perkins's dampened shoulder. "I don't, I won't!"

"I have been trying, Miss Trant, to convince her of the . . . the impropriety and the unreasonableness of our actions," said the haggard Mr. Perkins, all the while continuing to embrace Miss Beth with a great deal of protective fervor. "I do not know how I came to agree to make this mad journey, but I assure you nothing untoward has occurred between us. After our return to London, I shall, of course, not importune upon Miss Elizabeth further."

This noble speech had the effect of sending Miss Elizabeth's arms tightly about his neck, while the room reverberated with her fresh wails. At that moment the landlord shoved his way into the room and stood surveying them with arms akimbo.

"Here now! What's amiss? Such racket and goings-on at this time o'night!" He fixed narrowed eyes on Sir Charles with the look of a cock facing an opponent in a pit.

Quelling the man with one raised brow, Sir Charles remarked easily, "Don't be a fool, Perkins. Not to importune upon one's own wife would be beyond belief."

All weeping ceased as if snapped in two. "W-wife?" said Beth, venturing once more to peek over Josiah's shoulder.

One of the baronet's most dazzling off-center smiles crossed his face. "Wife," he repeated the instant before he turned his attention to the landlord. "Please instruct the ostlers to put your fastest, freshest team of four to the chaise outside and make ready for our immediate departure."

Obedient to the tones of one obviously used to giving

orders, the landlord scarcely hesitated to obey, though he shook his head as he left. As the door clicked shut behind him, a babble of voices assaulted the baronet.

"What can you mean, Charles?" Nell demanded.

"Sir, I beg you will cease to play your jests upon us," Perkins stated sourly.

"Do you mean, Sir Charles," Beth inquired, "that *you* do not wish to marry me?"

"It is not," returned Sir Charles gallantly, "that I would not wish to marry you, Miss Beth. But the world takes a dim view of a man having more than one wife."

"More than one . . . ?" Beth's bewilderment was abruptly transformed into a burst of joy. "Nell! Are you truly? Oh, that's truly wondrous news! I am so happy!"

She streaked in a flurry of pink to her sister's arms, where she was received with much laughter. "Yes, we are truly! I cannot quite think how it came about," Nell said with a glowing glance at her new fiancé, "but I have agreed to marry Sir Charles. And when we return to London, we shall convince Mama that you can marry only Mr. Perkins and no one else."

"Ahem." Sir Charles coughed diffidently. Three pairs of eyes settled on him as he said in the voice of one making a confession, "I rather feel I should tell you, my dear, that we are not returning to London just yet."

"What!" chimed all three voices in perfect harmony.

"It has occurred to me," explained the baronet as he slowly drew off his gloves, "that we should, after all, continue northward."

"Are you mad, sir?" Mr. Perkins inquired. "We cannot possibly place the ladies in such a scandalous position."

"Of course we are not going north," Nell said firmly. "He is only funning."

"*I*, for one, think the baronet is serious," Beth put in breathlessly, "and I am quite willing to go onward. I don't want Mama or Lord Harlowe or anyone putting a stop to my marriage!"

Sir Charles held his gloves in one hand and looked at them at last. A wicked determination sparkled in his sapphire eyes. The curve of his mouth was charming, yet steadfast. "I do not think you need fear your mother's rejection of Mr.

Perkins for you, Beth. Nor her condemnation of our elope-
ments."

"I agree with you, Mr. Perkins," Nell exclaimed. "He
is quite, quite mad."

Crossing with easy deliberation, Sir Charles took up
Nell's right hand, turned it in his own, and lightly laid his
lips on the inside of her wrist. "My lovely bride, do you
think your mother a fool? Why is it, do you think, that she
so often arranged for us to be alone?" With each question,
he dropped another kiss upon the pulsing vein of her wrist,
increasing its rate considerably. "Or that she wrote you as
she did when I asked for Beth? Had you not wondered why
she did not suffer the vapors this evening? And what, dear
heart, did you think she meant when she directed me to
settle this matter 'once and for all'?"

"I—I—oh, Charles, I cannot think—I can't," Nell floundered, curiously out of breath as she stared at the ebony
curls bending over her wrist. Inhaling deeply, she made a
valiant effort to finish. "It cannot be *right* for us to get
married over the anvil. Think what people will say."

"Hang the people!" Sir Charles said with one last flick
of his lips upon her now-furious pulse. He raised his head
and commanded her eyes with his darkly glittering gaze.
"I have been most . . . unfortunate, shall we say, in my be-
trothments. I do not intend to chance another, Nell. We go
on to Gretna Green."

"B-but the school." Nell faltered. In dismay, she heard
the hiss of his breath and saw pain cloud his eyes. An
anxious need to rid that hurt from him overwhelmed her.

"You can go back to your school or you can come with
me," Charles clipped out coldly. "If you want to marry me,
Nell, it's on to Gretna Green tonight."

The demand in both look and tone set Nell's heart to
fluttering wildly. Objections evaporated like morning mist.
She nodded and felt a ridiculous rapture shoot through her.

"Do you know, I've long felt that Drusilla is much better
suited to running the school than I. She loves it as I never
can. I shall give it to her as a . . . a wedding gift," Nell
pronounced. She was rewarded with a brilliant flash of love
in Sir Charles's eyes. Her skin tingled where his hand still
circled her slim wrist, and she thought surely he must feel

it. Two heavy raps upon the door broke the spell. Her wrist
gained unwanted freedom as Sir Charles straightened to face
the landlord. Their carriage, they were solemnly informed,
had been made ready.

"I must voice my protests to your outlandish scheme,
sir!" said Perkins, standing his ground despite Beth's insis-
tent tugging on his sleeve. "A double elopement! Why, it
passes all bounds!"

"I have ever been told, Mr. Perkins," stated the baronet,
"that I am one to set my own bounds. Come, either stay
and know you lost Beth to propriety, or join us and be
happily wed. I will not delay further." He cast his eyes over
the features of his bride-to-be and added softly, "I cannot
delay."

To her disgust, Nell blushed and trembled like the veriest
miss fresh out of the schoolroom. She put out a hand to Mr.
Perkins. "Josiah, we know you love Beth deeply, else you
would not have begun this journey. If we go on together,
we shall contrive to breeze through all that society may have
to say."

He seemed to hesitate, and suddenly Elizabeth's face
took on the cast of Medusa. "Pray, do not continue to plead
on my behalf, Nell! It is obvious to the least intelligence
that Mr. Perkins does not hold that regard for me that would
make a trip to Gretna Green of the least use."

"Beth! How can you say so? Of course I have that—that
regard for you!" protested Josiah. His attempts to take the
lady's hand were thoroughly spurned.

"Ha!" she said, leaving no doubt of her disbelief. "It is
*I* who should beg pardon for importuning upon *you*, sir! I
have dragged you here when your reluctance to wed me
could not be more plain!" She whirled away from him to
plant a tearful kiss upon her sister's cheek. "Good luck,
best of sisters! Do not, I beg you, worry about me. I shall
contrive to return home."

Her brave words faltered suspiciously. Mr. Perkins came
up behind her with her name spilling from his lips, but
before Beth could either accept or reject him, Sir Charles
took her chin and tilted it upward. He signaled Mr. Perkins
away with his other hand, then used it to gently wipe away
her flowing tears.

"You must consider very carefully what you are about, Beth. One injudicious word can bring a lifetime of misery. An argument that should never have been cost Nell and me three years of happiness. Do you want to suffer as we did? Think hard, child. You loved him enough to risk the scandal of elopement. Do you now wish to throw that away for a moment of pride?"

Her eyes glimmered up at him; her lips quivered. Very, very slowly, Beth shook her head.

"Darling," Josiah Perkins whispered hoarsely from behind her. "You must know how I love you! But how shall I support you? Lord Harlowe shall surely release me from his employment once this story is out. You would be wed to a penniless, out-of-work secretary. It is not the sort of life I would wish for you, my love."

"If that is all that has been forcing us to stand here for the past five minutes," Sir Charles said with a heavy sigh, "then for God's sake, let's not dally further. Perkins, I offer you a position at double—treble—your current salary, if you'll just take the chit and marry her!"

He narrowly escaped having his neck fervently wreathed by a grateful Elizabeth and his hand ardently wrung by her equally grateful fiancé. He did so by means of sweeping Nell within his arms and striding toward the door. Mr. Perkins was heard to utter one last word about impropriety as he and Beth followed them out.

"Hang the impropriety!" Sir Charles declared loudly, causing the inn's landlord to shake his head again.

"Hang the impropriety!" Nell echoed emphatically.

Their laughter carried softly on the night air.

# WATCH FOR
# 6 NEW TITLES EVERY MONTH!

## Second Chance at Love

## Second Chance at Love

### All of the above titles are $1.75 per copy

# WATCH FOR
# 6 NEW TITLES EVERY MONTH!

## Second Chance at Love™

_____ 05625-1 **MOURNING BRIDE #57** Lucia Curzon
_____ 06411-4 **THE GOLDEN TOUCH #58** Robin James
_____ 06596-X **EMBRACED BY DESTINY #59** Simone Hadary
_____ 06660-5 **TORN ASUNDER #60** Ann Cristy
_____ 06573-0 **MIRAGE #61** Margie Michaels
_____ 06650-8 **ON WINGS OF MAGIC #62** Susanna Collins
_____ 05816-5 **DOUBLE DECEPTION #63** Amanda Troy
_____ 06675-3 **APOLLO'S DREAM #64** Claire Evans
_____ 06676-1 **SMOLDERING EMBERS #65** Marie Charles
_____ 06677-X **STORMY PASSAGE #66** Laurel Blake
_____ 06678-8 **HALFWAY THERE #67** Aimée Duvall
_____ 06679-6 **SURPRISE ENDING #68** Elinor Stanton
_____ 06680-X **THE ROGUE'S LADY #69** Anne Devon
_____ 06681-8 **A FLAME TOO FIERCE #70** Jan Mathews
_____ 06682-6 **SATIN AND STEELE #71** Jaelyn Conlee
_____ 06683-4 **MIXED DOUBLES #72** Meredith Kingston
_____ 06684-2 **RETURN ENGAGEMENT #73** Kay Robbins
_____ 06685-0 **SULTRY NIGHTS #74** Ariel Tierney
_____ 06686-9 **AN IMPROPER BETROTHMENT #75** Henrietta Houston

All of the above titles are $1.75 per copy

# WHAT READERS SAY ABOUT
# SECOND CHANCE AT LOVE

"SECOND CHANCE AT LOVE is fantastic."
—*J. L., Greenville, South Carolina**

"SECOND CHANCE AT LOVE has all the romance of the big novels."
—*L. W., Oak Grove, Missouri**

"You deserve a standing ovation!"
—*S. C., Birch Run, Michigan**

"Thank you for putting out this type of story. Love and passion have no time limits. I look forward to more of these good books."
—*E. G., Huntsville, Alabama**

"Thank you for your excellent series of books. Our book stores receive their monthly selections between the second and third week of every month. Please believe me when I say they have a frantic female calling them every day until they get your books in."
—*C. Y., Sacramento, California**

"I have become addicted to the SECOND CHANCE AT LOVE books...You can be very proud of these books....I look forward to them each month."
—*D. A., Floral City, Florida**

"I have enjoyed every one of your SECOND CHANCE AT LOVE books. Reading them is like eating potato chips, once you start you just can't stop."
—*L. S., Kenosha, Wisconsin**

"I consider your SECOND CHANCE AT LOVE books the best on the market."
—*D. S., Redmond, Washington**

*Names and addresses available upon request